Mr.
DECEMBER

Michele Dunaway

Chapter One

"Up on the rooftop, reindeer paws . . ."

Or was it "pause"? As the chorus of impromptu Christmas caroling began—and it wasn't even Thanksgiving—Jack Donovan tugged at the annoying starched edge of his white shirt collar. Tuxedos were for proms and weddings—tonight was neither. He skirted the edge of the Chase Park Plaza's Khorassan Ballroom—supposedly the best in St. Louis—ignoring the two well-heeled women who gave him pointed looks before blushing and giggling.

Jack adjusted his black bow tie, wishing he could remove the required dress-code noose. While he really didn't have anywhere else to be, this was so not his scene. If the floor opened and swallowed him whole, he wouldn't mind. Maybe then he could also ditch the rented jacket that tightened every time he crossed his arms.

He eased into a corner, ensuring he was clear of the mistletoe sprigs hanging strategically between dangling strands of soft, tiny, white Christmas lights. He sipped from the brown long-necked bottle he'd been carrying for most of the evening, the King of Beers now lukewarm.

Celebratory cheers erupted as the carol reached its crescendo, and then the band resumed, much to Jack's relief. Christmas started earlier and earlier every year. Case in point, it was only seven days into November and some decorator had gone crazy with the holiday decorations: the ballroom was littered with poinsettias, miniature Christmas trees, silvery stars, glittery snowmen, and that damn mistletoe he'd been dodging all night.

He moved deeper into the shadows, edging around one of the almost life-size cutouts of the single men featured in the first Sexy Public Servants of St. Louis Charity Calendar. He'd known Joe Marino, firefighter and Mr. September, since Catholic youth soccer when they'd faced each other twice in the championship round. Now both were the faces of local charities, but while Joe seemed to relish the growing crowd of women, Jack wasn't thrilled with his sudden fame as Mr. December.

Unlike Joe, who'd at least gotten to wear turnout gear suspenders, pants, and coat in his photo, Jack wore only a Santa hat and low-rise jeans in his. Across the room a crowd of women added him to their Instagram accounts by surrounding and posing with the nearly naked cardboard version of Jack in all his holiday glory. Did one woman just paw his cardboard chest? Jack rolled his eyes heavenward. Great. More ammunition for his mother, the South Side's expert matchmaker. He loved his mother, but lately she had been harping on how he needed to find his soul mate, settle down, and start a family. She'd also been tossing women at him right and left. As the holiday season approached, she'd redoubled her efforts. Jack so far had avoided Susie Crenshaw, Alice Foster, and Laura Sims— who were all on his mom's current list of potential dates. All three had made a beeline for him earlier, clearly preprogramed to seek him out. As he'd signed Susie's calendar, she had slipped him her phone number.

Jack dangled the beer bottle between his fingertips and wished he could leave. What the hell had he been thinking, agreeing to all this? Oh yeah, his lieutenant had insisted, and one did not cross Lt. Steven Jones. Besides, Jack had been told, the calendar needed a cop, and as Jack was the face of the six-month-old St. Louis Police Department's Animal Cruelty Task Force, saying no hadn't been an option.

The publicity would be good exposure, he'd been assured. Considering the state of undress in Mr. December's photo, he'd been exposed all right. Thankfully, one-twelfth of the proceeds went to pet charities he'd been able to personally select so, at least some good would come out of his embarrassment. Even so, he couldn't help but grimace as some woman across the room tweaked his one-dimensional nipple and took a selfie; he prayed it was only a Snapchat that faded after a few seconds. As it was, his damn photo was already up on Google images, and two days ago the guys at the precinct had decorated his locker with hundreds of overlapping, baseball-card-size copies. It had taken a full twenty minutes to peel off the tape slivers.

A tall brunette caught his attention as she wove through the crowd, a long expanse of leg sliding through the thigh-high slit in her red dress. He didn't realize he was staring until she stood directly in front of him and held out her hand. "Hi," she said, her voice creating a shiver of awareness he hadn't felt in years. "You must be Jack. I'm Kat."

Damn. Talk about being caught off guard. He smiled automatically, as he'd been doing all night. "Hi."

Her fingers warmed under his, and he instinctively held on a second too long before letting go. Odd. "So someone"—she looked over her shoulder as if searching for that person—"told me you're the first member of the mayor's new task force."

"It says that in the calendar, yes."

Susie Crenshaw walked past, head swiveling as she searched for someone; Jack sank deeper into the shadows, closer to the emergency exit doors.

Kat noticed, and moved helpfully to block him. "Ex?"

Jack shook his head. "Nothing like that."

"Ah." Mirth lifted perfect lips, and her brown eyes twinkled. "One of your groupies. I saw how they fawned over you. Don't worry. You're safe with me."

Since his interest in the opposite sex had chosen this moment to reemerge, he wasn't so sure anyone was safe. That beautiful mouth begged to be kissed. He searched for a benign topic, then said the first thing that came to mind. "Did you buy a calendar? Did I already sign it?" He'd signed hundreds earlier during the group autograph session.

Although surely he would have remembered her. Those succulent red lips—lips that matched the color of her sleeveless velvet dress—wrapped around the edge of her champagne flute, and as she swallowed, Jack's underused libido flared to life. Brown hair up in a knot revealed a creamy white neck perfect for planting kisses on, and he longed to just that. He hardened.

"Ten of them actually and no, I'm good."

His eyebrows arched. Lost in trying to calm his lower half, had he heard her correctly? "You bought ten?"

She laughed, a light melodic sound that he wouldn't mind hearing over and over again. "It's for charity, and I'll give them to my staff."

She fingered the gold chain at her neck, and his gaze traced the filament down to where the jewelry dipped into the V of breasts caressed by hugging velvet. But with his mom's "Eyes up, Buster" admonition ingrained in his head since puberty, he focused on her face—and found brown eyes a man could drown in as he counted each little gold speck. And when those long brown lashes fluttered down . . . He swore his heart skipped.

Those red lips puckered humorously as she added, "Oh, and I can't forget a calendar for my grandmother, who's in a nursing home and says she's never too old to look. I'm sure she'll like your . . . Santa hat."

"And you?" The words popped out of his mouth, his genuine interest surprising him. He could practically hear his mother shout "Saints be praised!" For the past two years, ever since Julie ended their five-year relationship because of his commitment phobia, he'd felt not a flicker of interest. "How's your Christmas spirit?"

A rosy flush that matched her dress spread over her pale skin, momentarily distracting him. If the band played, he didn't hear it. Time seemed to freeze, if only for a second. "So?" he teased.

She shifted her weight, the revealing slit showcasing a long expanse of creamy mile-high leg his fingers itched to caress. Her mouth wrapped around the flute edge, and she took another long sip before replying. Underneath his jacket, Jack started to sweat. *Had someone turned up the heat?* "Well, everyone knows December is my favorite month. I love Christmas and everything that comes with it. . . ."

"Including Santa hats?"

"Maybe. I've been known to wear one or two when the occasion warranted."

That beautiful laugh trilled again, and those lashes fluttered down. Bright red painted nails toyed with her necklace, the color a seductive contrast against her pale skin. Desire to see her wearing nothing but heels and his hat made Jack lose his train of thought. Two years of nothing, not one iota or flicker of interest in the opposite sex, and suddenly—

"Jack! There you are!"

Jack winced at the familiar voice. Not only was Virginia Edwards Barker a doppelganger for a tad younger

Betty White, but the seventy-something socialite could rival Jack's grandmother in determination and grit in getting her way. She'd been bossing the calendar men around all evening.

"Looks like I'm needed," Jack said as the head of the charity calendar committee made a beeline for him. "Not that I wasn't enjoying this."

"Can we talk later?" Kat asked. Her fingers touched his arm. "I love animals. I'd like to get more involved and . . ."

Even through two layers of clothing he felt the searing of her touch, as if she'd branded his skin. Nerves short-circuited; his brain registered only the word *involved*. How many women tonight had asked him, "Are you involved with anyone? Would you like to be?" How many phone numbers had been thrust at him? He stepped backward, that distasteful word like a bucket of ice-cold water.

"Finally!" Virginia caught her breath and smoothed her taffeta gown. "It's taken me five minutes to find you. We're going to do a group photo for the paper. Did you forget?"

He never forgot anything, and his sharp mind was one reason he'd become a detective. He saw clues others missed and could recall them long after the fact. However, for a man who loved being in control, he had lost track of time and hated the idea of yet another picture. At least this time he'd be clothed. Jack faced Kat, those full red lips begging to be kissed, his emotions and memory a rare jumble. Maybe he had heard her wrong?

"Jack . . ." Virginia prompted.

"Kat—" he began, but before he finished, Virginia gave a delighted, joyous little clap. "Jack! Look up."

She pointed and Jack's gaze automatically followed, registering the mistletoe he'd been avoiding all night, especially after Alice Foster almost caught him underneath. Kat's deep brown eyes widened and her lush, inviting mouth formed a shocked O.

"Kiss, dear, it's tradition," Virginia commanded. She gave Kat a helpful push, and Jack drew her into an embrace, steadying her. His fingers sizzled as they touched her bare forearms. Then she wobbled on her stilettos and fell against his chest as a startled breath burst forth. His heart raced, and as need pulsed through him, he knew he had to taste her lips. Just one quick taste to get it out of his system . . .

The kiss lasted mere seconds, but even that one feathery touch sent a shockwave of desire to his already tight pants. He stepped back, having only a moment to register Kat's dazed expression before Virginia grabbed his arm and propelled him onward. "Find him after the photo, hon," she said. "You can reconnect then."

However, later, when Jack—despite his earlier intentions to escape—went to find Kat, she was gone.

***

Four weeks later

"'Tis the season to be jolly . . ."

Detective Jack Donovan's fingers tightened on the steering wheel of his SUV—a poor attempt to quell the urgent need to change the station to KSHE 95. All he had to do was press the button beneath his left thumb . . .

"Fa la la la la, la la la la!" his partner for the week chorused, his grin splitting ear to ear as the song finally ended. Jack hit the steering-wheel control and let out a contented sigh as Metallica's "Nothing Else Matters" started blaring through the speakers. "What? Tired of Christmas music?" Mike teased.

"It's only been playing since mid-October. "Tired" is an understatement." Jack glanced at the GPS then made a left turn.

Mike laughed. "Where's your holiday spirit, Scrooge? Mr. December needs to lighten up."

"Not happening. It's going to be a long thirteen months."

"What's wrong with representing Christmas? Or being famous?"

"Nothing." *Everything.* Jack bit back the rest of his retort. While he'd grown cynical, he wasn't rude. Besides, he'd known Mike since the academy, and high school before that. So although this was Mike's first ten-day stint on the Animal Cruelty Task Force, he could take liberties where others wouldn't dare—both men were equally ranked and good friends. "December's my least favorite month. Doing that calendar didn't help. Made me out to be a Christmas lover."

"Ha-ha. You are a witty scrooge." Mike slapped the dashboard. "And come on, admit you love all the women hanging up your photo and sending you fan letters. How many this week?"

"I don't. And one hundred and three. It's embarrassing. My mother also sees this as a grand opportunity to finally get me married. 'You're thirty,' she keeps harping. Thirty. As if that's the end of the world."

"Well, she isn't considered the neighborhood matchmaker for nothing. She helped me meet Suze, and we've got a baby on the way. And she's got your sister's wedding in a few weeks, and she just wants you happy . . ."

"Yeah, well, thank you for that dissertation Captain Obvious. I love my mom, but once she gets an idea in her head, she's as tenacious as a bulldog with a bone. I am not a project."

"That could be debatable," Mike returned. "And marriage is a good thing, buddy. Julie just wasn't your Mrs. Right. Whoever she is, I'm sure she's out there. You just have to find her."

"I don't have time," Jack replied, tightening his grip on the wheel as he turned into the alley. "So my mom's already searching for my wedding date."

"Maybe you need to date."

"I do not have time," Jack repeated.

"So find a temporary date," Mike suggested. "Someone you can just bring to the wedding to get your mom off your case."

"If you take any woman to a wedding, she gets the

wrong idea. And we're here." Jack threw the SUV into park, ending the annoying conversation. The only woman for whom he'd felt a flicker of interest had disappeared without a trace—not that he'd share that with Mike. "Eyes open."

Twenty feet ahead a small crowd had gathered behind a row of four-family apartment buildings. Jack's processing of a scene was such that he noticed everything, right down to the kid who wore sneakers so clean they had to be new. Had he bought them last night, when the stores had opened on Thanksgiving Day at six?

Now past noon on Black Friday, the amount of gawkers would actually make Jack's job easier as everyone was in one place to interview. "Ready?"

Mike nodded, drew a deep breath. "As I'll ever be."

"Your job is interviewing. Facts. Opinions. Anything we can use. I want to know what happened so I can arrest who did it."

"Got it."

Jack grabbed his camera. "And whatever you do, don't get sick."

"Sick?"

"You're about to find out why I hate December. Let's go."

Mike's eyes widened, but Jack slammed the door. Immediately his cop's senses cataloged everything, including a young boy around seven of mixed ethnicity who stood between him and the crowd. The boy looked Jack and Mike up and down, not intimidated by the fact that both men topped six feet. "You cops? You don't dress like cops."

"Well, we are." Jack indicated the silver badge attached to a leather belt that held up a worn pair of button-fly Levi's. His red flannel shirt and gray windbreaker were a testament to the unseasonably warm November weather. "But I work with animals."

The boy nodded, satisfied. "Pup's over there. He's Billy's dog. Got him as an early present last week."

"Early Christmas present?" Mike asked.

Fingers dug into back pockets. "Yeah. He'd always wanted a dog. Said his dad bought it for him."

The pounding started behind Jack's right eye. Giving animals as Christmas presents was always a bad idea. "Where does Billy live?"

The boy pointed a few buildings down the alley, and Jack made a mental note. "He lives on the second floor with his mom and aunt, and there's some others who come and go. You gonna arrest him?"

"Cops don't arrest innocent people."

"Marvin says you do."

Jack wasn't going to argue with Marvin—whoever he was. But he would arrest the guilty party, Jack determined. It was one of the reasons he'd accepted the job of heading up the St. Louis Police Department's Animal Cruelty Task Force. Animals were innocent, loving creatures, and he'd seen hideous things—burns, beatings, and hoardings— and with his memory he couldn't forget any of them. But he could honor those cruelly treated animals and ensure justice was done. Since June, he'd made eighteen arrests out of the sixty abuse cases he'd investigated.

The boy tagged along at Jack's heels as he approached the ten-deep crowd. His gaze took in each person, cataloging that they ranged from an elderly white woman to a well dressed but shell-shocked Asian woman. This area of South Side St. Louis was diverse and solidly middle class. A few people had decorated their back porches or balconies with strands of Christmas lights—the green cords visible although the lights were off.

The group parted like the Red Sea, and a five-foot-four woman with pure white hair clutched her terrycloth bathrobe between gnarled fingers. "Terrible," she kept repeating. "Terrible. Who would do such a thing?"

"We're going to find out," Jack promised. He squatted next to the overflowing neighborhood trash Dumpster. The 911 calls had reported an injured dog, but the information ended there. Between the back Dumpster wheel and the chain link fence lay a badly burned puppy, his brown fur pink and blistering.

Jack bit back an expletive, bile rising in his throat.

Behind him, Mike made a gagging noise; Jack forced down his earlier cheeseburger. As the lead investigator, he'd seen heinous things, but none like the horror before him.

Jack let the buzz of voices fade and concentrated only on the puppy's shallow breathing. A choke collar around its neck led to the metal leash attached to the fence. Black ash from an accelerant had charred the corner of the Dumpster and the ground. The dog opened deep brown eyes, long enough for Jack to feel as if a fist had squeezed his heart. No animal deserved this. "It's going to be okay, buddy," Jack told him as the dog whimpered. Then he barked out orders. "Mike, bolt cutters. Burn blanket. Call for backup."

Photos were essential for prosecution, especially if the animal died. *Although he was not going to let that happen to this puppy.* Not without doing everything possible.

"Get an arson investigator too," he called back.

He snapped several photos, making sure he had what he needed. Mike handed him the bolt cutters and he cut the dog loose and wrapped the dog gently in the blanket. He would make whoever did this pay.

"Unit's two blocks over. Rescue group is about fifteen minutes out," Mike said.

The puppy whimpered again, and Jack's fury grew. "I can't wait that long. What partner clinic's closest?"

Mike hit a button on his phone. "Checking."

"Watcha gonna do?" the boy asked.

"Take the puppy to the vet." Jack stood and cradled the bundle to his chest. "Can you assist Officer B?" After shortening his partner's name, Jack paused for the boy to supply his. "Peter. I'm Peter," he said helpfully.

"Nice to meet you Peter. You can be a hero, okay? Just show Officer B where Billy lives so I can take care of his dog. I want to make sure this puppy lives."

"Me too." Peter's head bobbed. "I can do that. He was a good dog."

A white police cruiser with flashing lights but no siren churned gravel as it parked behind the SUV. Two uniformed officers jumped out.

"Chippewa Animal Clinic," Mike said.

"Aren't they having legal issues? I got a complaint letter about an unpermitted shelter and dogs in their own waste."

"They passed the application and site visit with flying colors three weeks ago. Jeff did the inspection. The vet clinic is aboveboard. And it's practically right around the corner."

Jack touched the dog, avoiding its singed skin. The dog's shallow heartbeat made him deeply protective. Timing was crucial. He'd already planned on investigating Monday. "Call and tell them I'm inbound, and cancel the rescue group. While I'm gone, start processing the scene. I'll be right back."

One of the uniformed officers took one look at the dog's blistering face, and his own blanched. He covered his gagging mouth with a hand. "Jesus."

The dog trembled as Jack placed him tenderly in the cage in the back of the SUV. "Yeah. Some kid's early Christmas present."

The patrolman's face grew red. "Some people deserve to go to hell."

Jack couldn't agree more.

***

Kat Saunders reread the legal notice before turning the offensive missive over, as if the plain backside of the cream-colored paper would magically erase the mess she found

15

herself in.

When she'd bought the Chippewa Animal Clinic five years ago, she'd used all of her savings and even secured a hefty loan to purchase the business, which was grandfathered into a well-established and sought-after neighborhood. Houses in St. Louis Hills were some of the most coveted on the South Side.

Problem was, she had the occupancy permits to run a veterinarian practice but not the ones necessary for the no-kill shelter now also occupying the premises. She'd never intended to run a shelter; a couple years ago she'd taken in a few strays until she could find new owners. Then there were a few more. And then a few more—up until recently, no one had complained.

Now she was the subject of a neighborhood association witch hunt. Her clinic's reputation was under attack, as well as Kat personally. The association, led by Fred Fennewald, had complained about almost everything. She'd been investigated for noise violations—when the dogs were outside in the yard, Fred maintained they were too loud and disturbed the neighborhood. The association had filed a suit against her—stalling the permit process. Fred had alerted a newspaper reporter, and while the story had been factual, the online comments had contained lies saying she didn't care for her animals. They'd insinuated she kept them standing in filth, that she starved them. Kat had lost several clients as a result. She didn't know what she'd done to make Fred so disagreeable. Her clinic was her life's dream—she'd sacrificed everything to make this place work, including her nest egg. Now she needed a miracle to keep the city's zoning board from shutting the shelter down. If it closed, where would the homeless animals go? She was all in. Her parents—both doctors—had thought she'd follow in their footsteps, but she'd forged her own path. She couldn't back down now. Her vet tech Angela poked her head in. "Your phone's on silent."

"Again?" How many times a day did she accidentally push the button on the cordless receiver? "What's up?"

"The animal task force called," Angela said. "Our first case is on its way."

Kat's heart jumped erratically, and her gaze drifted to the stack of ten charity calendars sitting on a bookshelf. Since the ball, she'd admittedly peeked at Jack Donovan a few times. While sculpted abs, low-rise black jeans, and nothing but a Santa hat oozed sex appeal, he was devastatingly handsome in a tux. When she approached him at the gala, he looked like a slightly pissed-off James Bond. He'd had great hair—a shaggy blond mane that she'd itched to touch—an urge she'd blamed on two glasses of champagne. *And that kiss!* Suddenly she'd been too hot, and the band's next song—urging heated revelers to take off all their clothes—had hit a little too close to home.

"What's incoming?" she asked, forcing a focus on the professional. The kiss had been a momentary lapse—a stupid romantic fantasy of a career woman who had too little time and a bad dating track record to boot.

"Dog with burns on at least half its body."

Kat winced and rose, court summons forgotten. She

listened as her tech outlined the extent of the dog's injuries. It was clear that the rescue group doing the transport needed the nearest vet. "ETA?"

"Five minutes max. Claire's prepping the O.R."

"Make sure we're ready."

"We will be. I told them to use the emergency entrance."

Kat stepped from her office into the waiting room, the aromatic scent of a real Christmas tree greeting her. She'd spent Thanksgiving morning decorating the clinic, and Christmas music played over the speakers. "Silent Night," her favorite.

To her, there was nothing better than picking out a Christmas tree, and she'd bought hers down the street at Ted Drewes, a St. Louis landmark. The store located on Old Route 66 had been at the location since 1941, serving frozen custard in the summer and selling balsam fir trees from Nova Scotia in the winter. The owner picked them out himself. As for the frozen custard, a micro-chip concrete was her favorite.

She greeted a few patients who waited to see her associate, Dr. Stuart Marshall. She noted that there was fresh coffee and plates filled with Christmas cookies for both humans and dogs—separate, of course. Her staff had everything under control, and they'd keep it that way.

Flickering red and blue lights reflected through the large picture window as a black SUV pulled into the lot and headed around the side of the building. Adrenaline pumped in Kat's veins, and she took a deep breath. Her white lab coat flapped as she strode into the back of the clinic. Since she loved animals, joining the task force as a partner had been a logical step, especially since the new task force needed a partner clinic in her area. Jeff Ellis of Pet Rescue had spent three months vetting her clinic. She'd trained for this. She wouldn't fail.

She'd donned her green surgical gear and scrubbed in by the time the man carrying the dog entered her operating room.

"Hey sweet baby," she cooed, her gaze on the suffering dog.

"Hey to you too."

Kat's head jerked up. She knew that deep-timbered, rough-sounding voice. Six-feet of blond all-American hero stood there, his windbreaker askew. *Where was the rescue group?* "You," she sputtered. Mr. December, the man whose kiss sent tingles to her feet, stood in front of her.

"Me." He gently placed the dog on the stainless steel table. "And thanks for such a sweet greeting. Don't usually get that."

"I was talking to the dog," Kat clarified, all business. He didn't need to know how he'd made her body react. "I was expecting the rescue group."

Jack's lips formed a thin line. "Too bad. I could use some babying after this. There was no time to wait. How bad is he?"

Aware of her staff's avid curiosity, Kat's fingers peeled back the blanket to find what appeared to be a five-month-old pit bull puppy. Sweet, hopeful brown eyes tore at her heartstrings. "Shh," she urged, and the dog closed its eyes, the pain unbearable.

"Can you save him?" Jack asked.

"I'm going to try my best." Her brain registered and then dismissed her horror and anger. The puppy was going into shock—she didn't have time for distracting emotions. While she'd expected to see Jack Donovan at some point during her volunteering for the task force, she hadn't expected to be blindsided like this. She'd envisioned their next encounter at a training seminar or a meeting, or something . . . sometime when she'd be polished. Wearing makeup.

Her staff moved around her, getting things prepared. Work called. "I need you to leave," she told Jack.

He hesitated, his beautiful blue eyes imploring, holding her gaze. The world seemed to drop away, as if they were the only two in it. "I'm going to save him," she promised. "But I can't do that unless you leave."

The moment Jack left the room, Kat exhaled the breath she hadn't known she'd been holding. Twice now Mr. December's calendar image failed to do him justice. Twice now she'd felt the heat that radiated between them. Even being stressed and obviously tired hadn't lessened his magnetic, innate appeal.

If anything, today proved he had a deep, caring heart as well; he'd carried the dog and brought the animal himself. Mr. December certainly had far more layers than his objective photo revealed, layers she wanted to explore. Later. Much later.

After she saved this dog. This is why she'd signed up to volunteer, why she'd built the shelter. To save animals. Seeing Mr. December was not going to throw her off her game. "Let's get you fixed up," she said to the puppy, and got to work.

Chapter Two

Even after an hour on the hard bench, the growing backache was the least of Jack's discomforts. Once he'd dropped off the puppy, he'd rejoined Mike at the crime scene, and together they'd interviewed neighbors and various onlookers.

They'd also met with Billy, who was devastated over the loss of his dog. His mom had been at work, but his aunt has been babysitting and "consoling" Billy by telling him that real men didn't cry. She'd told Mike and Jack that it was probably for the best, as the dog had bit a younger cousin. Jack hadn't liked the petite blond much. He'd left after telling Billy he'd be back to talk to his mother.

Upon his return to the clinic, Jack was encouraged to hear the puppy was still in surgery. Had the puppy's condition been hopeless, he figured Kat would have euthanized.

So Jack waited, for aside from finishing and filing his report, there was really little else he could do. One or two pet owners had recognized him and mentioned the calendar, but they'd simply been friendly and somewhat curious, and he'd been able to disengage from the conversations without being offensive.

The clinic staff was another matter. He'd been getting quite a few sideways glances from the front-desk staff, especially over the last fifteen minutes. When he'd caught one staring, she'd even blushed. Had their boss told them about the kiss that was now plaguing his thoughts?

Jack tapped his fingers on the smooth surfaces on each side of his MacBook Pro's silver track pad, a clear sign of agitated nerves. He rubbed his right temple, for—despite two ibuprofen—his head pounded. The barking dogs and that annoying Christmas music didn't help. He stretched out his legs, leaned back, rubbed the end of his nose to stop the annoying twitch, and reminded himself his suffering was nothing compared to that of Case Number 63, the burned puppy, now in the hands of the woman whose kiss had roared back into his memory the moment he'd walked into her O.R. and seen her standing there like an angel in scrubs.

He hadn't forgotten her—he didn't forget anything—but he hadn't been able to dismiss her. His memory was such that when given a date or an incident, he relived it. He could feel the clothes he wore, experience a soft touch, even smell the perfume. Now it was as if he was there all over again—the sensations all rushing back.

Now here she was, the woman who'd gotten under his skin, who'd bothered him since that impromptu kiss under the mistletoe. He'd wondered who she was—he'd read over the guest list and not found Kat's name.

He'd gone back into his memory, searching for clues but finding none. That action only incited his subconscious to give her a staring role in one particularly graphic dream, making him wake up in a hot sweat. That fact had bothered him most of all. He was not a randy fifteen-year-old who couldn't control his hormones.

His e-mail popped up a message from the Public Affairs officer that a local media outlet had caught hold of the story and a news crew would be arriving at any time.

Jack closed his laptop and resisted the urge to Google Kat and her clinic, now that he had a somewhat free moment. Instead he closed his eyes and leaned his head against the wall. *Why was it always pit bulls?* Once known and loved for their gentle dispositions—Helen Keller had a pit bull—now the worst of humanity raised them for dogfighting or home protection, giving the entire breed a bad name. From his own experience he knew there weren't any bad dogs, just bad owners. In this case, neighbors and Billy's aunt had told him the dog had bitten several people. After further questioning, Billy's aunt had admitted the dog had been provoked into biting. The kids had been playing rough, teasing the dog by showing it a toy, letting him have it a second, and then yanking it away. Puppies don't understand jokes.

Jack made a fist then unclenched it, the movement diffusing his anger. Based on the initial investigation, he was 95 percent certain who'd done it. Soon he'd have solid proof, enough irrefutable evidence for an airtight arrest warrant and hopefully a subsequent conviction. Under the emergency warrant a judge had granted twenty minutes ago, the police force's finest computer hacker was on the case; so Jack opened his eyes, lifted the laptop lid, and filed the report via the secure web portal.

"Can I get you anything?" He tilted his head; one of the front-desk women stood there. Like everyone at the practice, she wore scrubs. She gestured to the refreshment table. "We have fresh coffee and cookies. I'd be happy to grab you a cup. You look tired."

He was, not that he'd admit it. His stomach growled, and he assumed the cookies with the chocolate chips were for humans. He held up the insulated paper cup he'd grabbed earlier at the local gas station. "Thanks, but I'm good. I'll grab something later if I change my mind. Do you know how much longer?"

Her smile was apologetic. "I'm sorry. I have no idea. We close at five, but you're welcome to stay after. I'm sure Dr. Saunders will want to talk with you."

"And me with her. Thanks."

He finished the cold coffee, eyed the cookies again, and decided he didn't feel like moving. He gave into curiosity and entered Kat's name into his web browser's search bar.

By the time Kat appeared ten minutes past five, not only was he the only one left in the waiting room aside from the staff, but he also knew everything about Kat—Katherine—Saunders.

"You're still here," she said.

"Yeah." He rose, noting she'd changed. She wore a clean white lab coat with *Dr. Katherine Saunders, DVM* embroidered in blue over her heart. She'd secured her brown hair into a messy ponytail, and brown eyes with gold flecks didn't hide that she'd been through a shell-shocking experience. He had the sudden urge to give her a big hug, to tug her against him. "How is he?"

She thrust her hands into her coat pockets, the fabric stretching over her breasts. "Three cracked ribs from where he was probably kicked multiple times. Burns on fifty percent of his body caused by an accelerant, my guess gasoline. Stable, for now, but the next twenty-four hours will tell if he'll pull through. But for now he's alive."

Her full lower lip quivered, and Jack quelled the need to take his forefinger and explore the texture. Even without a stitch of makeup she was beautiful, and the jolt of desire he felt surprised him, as did his overpowering need to comfort her, to take care of her. "Thank you. I know this is probably not what you signed up for."

"All in a day's work." Kat's quip fell flat, and her brown eyes misted.

"Come here." Jack pulled her into his arms, where she fit as if made for him. For a moment she nestled her head on his chest, and it felt heavenly. He had a sudden flash of being in bed, cuddled together after a long night of lovemaking. His hold tightened, and she bit back a sniffle. "People can be real assholes," he said gruffly.

Realizing where she was and what she was doing, Kat

pulled away and Jack let her go, not sure if he was disappointed or relieved.

She crossed her arms, her tough professional exterior dropping in place. Her anger grew and she scowled. "Just tell me you'll get whoever did this."

Jack's jaw tightened, and the throbbing behind his eye returned. "Trust me. That's my promise. I will get the person who did this."

"Dr. Saunders?"

As her receptionist approached, Kat's cheeks flushed. Her front-desk employees had just watched her hug Mr. December. Could they tell how much she wanted more? "Yes?"

"We have company," Louise, her receptionist, said.

A movement out the picture window captured everyone's attention as a news van pulled into the parking lot. Kat's face paled. "What are *they* doing here?"

"They got hold of the story. You're the one who treated the dog. They'll want to talk to you," Jack said.

She dug her fingers into his arm. "You don't understand. I can't. I don't want the publicity."

"Ow!" Jack stepped back, massaged where she'd touched. That wasn't the reaction he'd been expecting. "Why not? It'll be good for your clinic and for the task force. You saved the day. You deserve some credit. Happy press."

As a news reporter and cameraman climbed out and made their way to the front door, panic clawed at Kat. Her lawyer had said that she needed to keep a low profile. Do nothing—nothing—that would bring unnecessary attention. Being on the local news wasn't considered discreet.

The glass door squeaked open, and a two-man crew entered. "Jack," the reporter greeted, shaking Jack's hand. "How are you?"

"Had better days." Jack said. "Anthony, this is Dr. Katherine Saunders. She saved a puppy today—one of the worse animal abuse cases I've ever seen."

"Tell me what happened, but first . . ." Anthony handed Jack a wireless microphone. The camera light flashed red for Record. "Okay, go."

Jack began to speak. "Today I received a call about a pit bull puppy with burns on over fifty percent of his body. I brought him here . . ."

As Jack explained the situation to the reporter, Kat marveled at the difference. While he'd been obviously uncomfortable the night of the ball with the attention he'd received, he was a pro at being interviewed.

"He's hotter in person," Angela whispered. All of Kat's employees had gathered around.

That's an understatement, Kat thought. Jack spoke strong and sure, his deep timbered voice the type the media loved. Earlier, when he'd simply given her a hug, she'd thought she might short circuit. But, like that kiss, all that heat meant nothing. "Don't you all have work to do?" Kat hissed at Angela.

"Fine. Let's go ladies," Angela called, softly enough so camera wouldn't pick up. She and the rest of the staff went into the back to do the evening feedings. Kat took a breath. She didn't want an audience for the interview.

"Your turn," Jack said when finished. He held out the microphone. Behind him, the reporter and cameraman conferred.

Kat's nerves stretched. "I don't want to do this."

"Publicity is an important aspect of the task force."

"Says the guy who was hiding in a corner the night of the gala."

The edges of his lips puckered. Clearly she'd hit a nerve. "The media is essential for getting the public on our side. The mayor took a lot of flack for dedicating an officer specifically to animal crimes. Some see it as a waste of taxpayer dollars. Media is a necessary evil. The calendar— that's my superior officer's brainchild and one I couldn't refuse."

The small black metal box felt heavy in Kat's hand. "You've probably had media training."

"Yes, but you'll do fine. Just speak the truth. Let me get you wired." He stepped into her space, his six-foot bulk towering over her. The stilettos she'd worn the night of the ball had made her his height; in her work shoes she stood only five eight.

"This goes here." He clipped the mic to her lapel. Then he moved her lab coat aside and hid the thin cord underneath, the movement draping the cord so it skimmed the outer edge of her left breast. Her breath caught, and he held out the transmitter. "Tuck that into your back pants pocket."

"At least you aren't doing *that* for me."

Blue eyes glittered. "I can if you want."

"No, I'm good," Kat said, heart racing.

"You ready?" the cameraman asked. "We're trying to hit the six p.m. broadcast."

"Ready," Kat replied, following Anthony's gesture to stand in front of the Christmas tree.

"This'll be a good backdrop," Anthony said. Kat forced herself to relax, and when prompted, spoke about the extent of the puppy's injuries and how the next twenty-four hours would be crucial.

"So what else do you do in cases like this?" Anthony asked.

Kat blinked. "I've never seen a case this horrendous. I will be staying on site tonight to make sure Jingle pulls through."

"Jingle?" Anthony asked.

Kat jutted her chin forward. "There was a small bell attached to his choke collar, and he deserved a new name, one that reflected holiday spirit and optimism. *It's a Wonderful Life* is one of my favorite movies."

"So every time an angel gets his wings, a bell rings," Anthony clarified.

"That's the movie," she confirmed. "Christmas is a time for miracles."

"So are you going to be Jingle's guardian angel?"

"I am going to do my very best."

"Great. Jingle it is. The viewers will love that." Anthony grinned. "That's all I need except to film him."

Her ponytail swished as she shook her head. "Absolutely not. He needs rest and to be left alone. Not to mention, it's a sterile environment."

Jack spoke up, asserted control. "Contact Public Affairs and see what they're willing to share. I submitted photos with my report."

"I'll do that. Thanks so much for your time, Dr. Saunders. You can take your mic off, and I'll film the rest of my segment from outside. I might be here awhile if that's okay. Producers may want to have me live on location with your clinic as a backdrop."

"I—"

"That's fine," Jack interrupted, anticipating Kat's refusal. "Dr. Saunders will be happy to help the task force out in any way possible, won't you?"

She unclipped the mic and passed it to the cameraman. Anthony handed her his business card, unaware of Kat's growing tension. "We'll run the story at six and ten. The full version will be online. You will call me if there are any changes? Our viewers will want to know how he's doing. This type of story always tugs the heartstrings, so there will be multiple follow-ups. Remember Trooper, the dog dragged behind the car?"

"Jingle is not ratings material," Kat said stiffly. "Jingle's an injured dog."

Jack cupped her elbow in warning. "No, he's not, but the public will be compelled to do something. They'll be moved to call in other abuse. They'll donate money toward his care, and Pet Rescue maintains a specific account dedicated to task force causes. Think of all the animals Jingle can help, all the good that can come out of this horrible situation."

"Fine." Kat conceded and tucked the card into her lab coat pocket as the media left. Her staff was in the back, checking on the animals. By six, everyone would be gone, off to their Friday night activities. Kat forced herself to relax. The 24-7 Christmas radio station began to play "Joy to the World," another of her favorites, and she automatically began to hum along, until she realized Jack remained in the room, staring at her.

"You don't need to stay," she told him.

"I wanted to give you my card." He proffered a slip of paper, and she placed the white cardstock with the other one. "I also wanted to talk to you."

She kept her tone bright, unaffected. "Why?"

He shifted his weight, shoved his hands into front jeans pockets. "You don't make things easy, do you?"

She scowled. "No woman wants to be easy."

"No woman should be difficult, either."

Her last serious boyfriend had used that word during their final fight. Kat's hands went on her hips. "You don't know me. I do not appreciate—"

"I'm sorry," he cut in. "I'm not handling this well. I'm not trying to offend you. But the kiss . . ."

"It was just a kiss. Caused by mistletoe. Nothing to stress about," she replied, using her best nonchalant tone. No need for him to know she'd searched for him. No need for him to realize his perfect lips had rocked her world. Or that she'd fantasized about being in his arms. *And in his bed.*

"Well, it shocked me seeing you today. If I reacted poorly, I apologize. I never intended to make you uncomfortable." He stepped forward. Stopped short. A hand raked his hair off his forehead, and then the blond strands simply returned to their previous position. "I couldn't have saved him without you."

"You helped by letting me cut off his collar, rather than cutting it off yourself on site," she admitted.

He gestured. "So, square?"

"I guess. It shocked me not to see the rescue group doing the transport like the procedure manual says would happen. But every second counted. Your efforts made the difference."

"Look, can I buy you dinner? I . . ."

"Thanks, but no. Best we keep this relationship professional." As she shook her head, she realized multiple strands had escaped her ponytail and she probably looked like something the cat dragged in.

"You need to eat."

His kindness and concern touched her. "True, but I'll order delivery. Lots of places around here to chose from. I'm thinking Thai."

A blond eyebrow arched. "You're really going to sleep here?"

"It wasn't a line. I'm set up for just such contingencies," she replied, her tone confident. Kat pointed to a camera hanging up in the corner of the room. "I have eyes everywhere and a state of the art security system. I'll be fine.

Besides, the police substation is right down the block."

"True." Jack's weight shifted again.

She worked to reassure him so he'd feel free to leave. "Tonight is crucial. It's best for me to be here. If something goes wrong, time is of the essence."

"Can I call you later to check on how he's doing?"

"The phones will roll to voice mail."

"I could go get carryout, wait with you. Keep you company," he offered, enticing her.

Company would be nice, especially his, but somehow she resisted. "Really, I'm fine. I'll call you if anything changes." She patted her pocket. "Promise."

The moment stretched, as Jack clearly wanted to say more.

"Go enjoy your weekend," she told him before her resolve faltered. The man was temptation personified. "I'm sure you have places to go, people to see. Don't let me keep you. As for me, I still have work to do, including checking on Jingle."

Jack had absolutely no plans aside from turning on his TV and watching the Blues take on the Blackhawks, but he kept that to himself. He also wanted to ask about her shelter, but given that Jeff Ellis of Pet Rescue had approved her clinic, he knew it could wait until tomorrow. Jeff was the city's most outspoken animal advocate and the man who'd singlehandedly convinced the mayor to form the task force. He thought of the letter he'd read. After meeting Kat, his gut told him something about the letter was off.

"No matter what time, call me and I can be here," he told her. "I need to be here, if—"

"I understand," she said crisply, keeping the professional mask firmly in place. Jack's offer to buy dinner and keep her company had sent sweet little tingles to her toes. She wanted to see more of him but knew she had to be professional. Her head—and the rest of her—were battling. Time to get him to a safe distance. "Don't worry. I will make sure nothing happens to him now that he is in my care."

He nodded at her conviction. "No, it probably won't. I can tell you keep your word."

"Exactly." Her countenance softened. She liked how persistent he was, how passionate. "We open tomorrow at nine. We close again at four. My staff—"

"While I'll call first thing, I'll want to see him for myself," Jack interrupted. "I'll come by tomorrow. I'll be checking on him personally for as long as it takes, pretty much until he's adoptable. For the foreseeable future, you and I will be seeing a lot more of each other."

He reached out, touched her cheek with the back of his forefinger. A shiver of anticipation shot through her. "Until tomorrow, Kat."

Then he was gone. As she locked the backdoor and watched him climb into his SUV, Kat knew she could take Jack's final words to the bank. Her cheek tingled. She reached up, traced her cheek where he'd branded her with the lightest of touches. Jingle would take a while to heal, which meant Jack Donovan was about to be in her life for a long time. *A very, very long time.*

"Merry Christmas to me," she whispered, and went to check on her patient.

Chapter Three

By the time Jack appeared around noon, Kat's nerves had stretched thin from anticipation.

"You're being silly," she mumbled to herself. "Stop it."

They were professional colleagues, if that. Certainly nothing more, which didn't explain the giddy feeling she'd gotten when to she'd spoken with him briefly first thing this morning.

And the moment her tech had poked her head into the office and said, "Mr. December's just pulled in," Kat's stomach had fluttered with thousands of butterflies. Certainly not a professional reaction. More like her teenage, silly self—an often-heartbroken girl she didn't mind leaving behind.

Jingle had made it through the night and, thankfully, remained stable. She'd kept the puppy on intensive painkillers delivered directly to his bloodstream along with intravenous fluids. She kept him sedated so he slept, his body's natural healing mechanism for warding off infection.

"How is he?"

"Still in intensive care, but I'm very hopeful," Kat answered as Jack strode into her office like he owned the place, white paper bag in hand.

"No, don't get up." He dropped into the chair in front of her desk and glanced around, as if noting the very comfy couch she always slept on, her degree from the University of Missouri, various knickknacks and books, and the family photo on the bookshelf where the stack of calendars had been. Kat had put *those* in a desk drawer. He set the bag on her desk. Delicious smells reached her nose.

"I stopped at Salume Beddu. Since you ate dinner by yourself, I thought I might tempt you to join me for lunch if I brought the right incentive. Your staff said you had about an hour."

Her mouth watered. Considered one of St. Louis's top sandwich venues, the artisan specialty shop cured its own meats. "What did you order?"

"Wasn't sure if you were vegetarian or not, so I brought a Beast, a Speck, and one of their roasted vegetable with mozzarella. Figured whatever you didn't want, I could reheat and eat tomorrow."

The Beast was a fresh sausage sandwich with roasted hot peppers and onions. "I don't eat a lot of meat, but I do when the occasion warrants. The Speck will be perfect." That was thinly sliced, cured Italian pork topped with lemons and Gruyère cheese.

"A woman after my own heart," he said, passing her

sandwich over.

"Or at least your food." She reached behind her, took out two waters from the dorm-size refrigerator next to her desk. She handed him one, their fingers connecting with a zing over the cold bottle. She snapped her head up, their gazes colliding. For one brief moment she imagined how his electrified hands would feel on other parts of her body. Blushing, she looked away and cleared her throat. "I'll make up for the calorie splurge by eating a salad later."

He held up a hand. "No. Don't tell me that. I like a woman who eats." He began to unwrap his sandwich. "Do you know how many women pick at their food and push it around their plates? I don't know what they hope to accomplish."

"Smaller hips?"

"Well, whatever the reason, those types of women annoy me. A woman with an appetite is sexy."

She uncapped her bottle and took a long drink. The cold water rushing down her throat did nothing to ease the sexual charge.

"So, date a lot of those women?"

"My fair share," he admitted as strong fingers tore his sandwich in half. "Then I wised up. Told my mother I'd find my own dates."

Kat laughed. "Your mother fixes you up?"

"She's the neighborhood matchmaker. She fixes everyone up. She claims I'm a lost cause, but she refuses to quit."

He inserted a finger into his mouth and licked off the

residual sauce. Kat tore her gaze from those sensual lips. "This is so good," he said.

"It is," she agreed, taking her own bite.

He grinned, and she could feel his charm as if it were a hand pulling her close. "Well I'm glad I made the right choice."

"Me too. Better than my salad." She took another bite and moaned with pleasure. "I should go there more often."

"You should," Jack replied, his attention fully on Kat's enjoyment. He hadn't lied about those women. Julie had always complained she'd be fat if she ate so and so or such and such. Once they'd broken up, he'd dated now and then, but had easily found deal breakers every time.

But Kat . . . she dug into the sandwich with gusto. No, he thought, that wasn't the right term. She wasn't slovenly or sloppy like those cops in his division who could wolf down a sandwich or burger in seconds flat. However, clearly she enjoyed the experience of eating. He'd grown up in a household where mealtimes were family events, the food savored and appreciated.

She licked her lips, and Jack's libido roared to life as he imagined what it would be like to kiss her again, to taste her mouth fully. . . . He tore himself from those dangerous thoughts. The erotic dreams already teased his memory. "I appreciate good food. My mom is a terrific cook. She makes enough for an army every Sunday, and if I'm free, I go over. Lately, though, it's all about my sister—well, stepsister. She's getting married in December. Even though it's a delicious home-cooked meal, it's all wedding this, wedding that. . . . Sorry, I'm probably boring you."

"No, you're not. It sounds wonderful. My parents were the kings of takeout. Still are, actually. My mom works full time—she's a doctor—so she never cooked much. She did bake, though." Kat set the sandwich down, taking a momentary break. "Again, excellent choice. This is so good."

Her lips puckered as she drew out the O in *so,* and a warm, fuzzy—and strange—feeling bloomed in his chest. "Then I'm glad I took a risk. It was that or the King and I on Grand, but last night you said you were going to do Thai."

"This is perfect."

He took another bite and swallowed, struck by the thought that she was pretty perfect herself. Perhaps that's why he hadn't yet broached the complaint letter in his pocket. "So you said Jingle needs intensive care, but can you be more specific?"

"He's sedated but not out of the woods. I'm watching for fever, shock, infection . . ." She opened the bag of chips that had come with her sandwich. "A lot of his recovery comes down to fate and his own will to live."

"I hope it's strong."

She nodded. "Me too."

"I'd like to see him."

"I'll take you back."

"Perfect. I do need to take a few more pictures. I also want to see your shel— Hey!" Jack jumped up as a ball of oversize gray fluff landed on the chair arm. "What the?"

A wide pair of green cat eyes held his gaze without blinking. "Hey cat." He settled back into his seat, feeling a bit sheepish. "You scared me."

Kat was trying hard not to laugh. "Just stop," he told her as he picked up his napkin from the floor. "I can hear your thoughts. Mr. Big Bad Police Officer got scared by a cat."

"Never," Kat said, but her brown eyes twinkled. "That's Crystal. You're in her spot."

"Sorry cat." The cat licked its paw as if Jack wasn't even there.

"She knows she's being bad, so just nudge her a bit. She won't mind."

The soft gray feline leaned closer, nose twitching as she investigated the sandwich Jack had placed on Kat's desk. He moved his lunch into his left hand, and the cat leaned across his lap, all four paws perfectly balanced on the three-inch edge of the chair.

"Crystal!" Kat admonished. The cat straightened, flicked its tail, and jumped down. "I'm so sorry about that. She's being nosy and rude. She won't eat people food."

"I thought all animals did."

"No. That's a myth. Had you torn off a piece of meat or cheese, she would have just sniffed it and then ignored it. The idea is that she made you give it to her. That makes her dominant cat."

"So I lost to a cat?"

Kat started to giggle; the sound amused him. "You did. Sorry."

"No, you're not."

She shook her head, laughed. "No, I'm not."

"So much for me being an animal genius." Because her smile lit up her whole face, he couldn't help but laugh, too, even though the jest was on him. Joking with her created warm, happy feelings, the kind he'd been missing for two years. The letter burned a hole in his pocket; he'd broach the shelter topic again, but later. "Learn something every day. So do you take her back and forth?"

"She lives here. I have three of them wandering around, and Crystal's the boss. They have the run of the place but we cage them at night for safety reasons. I'd have more but the city . . . Do you have pets?"

A wave of blond hair fell into his face. He brushed it back, the gesture rote. He should cut it, but as he'd hated the buzz cut of the academy, he'd sworn he'd never, ever, go that direction again and never had. "No. No pets."

A wrinkle formed between her eyebrows, and he itched to smooth it. "That's a surprise."

He tore off some of the bread. "I love pets. But I'm not around enough to care for them. I deal all day with neglected animals. I can't sit in judgment over another if I'm irresponsible myself."

"Not even a cat? Those are pretty self-sufficient, especially if you have two that get along. They entertain each other. You do like cats, don't you?"

"I do." He opened his bag of chips, which rustled as he withdrew some. Crystal put up a paw, touched his arm. "You don't get any," he told her.

"Crystal," Kat commanded, but it was clear to Jack that Crystal was dominant where Kat was concerned, too. Now he didn't feel so bad.

"There are days I'm gone almost twenty-four hours. Last winter, remember that foot of snow and the subzero temperatures we got? What was it, the polar vortex or something?"

"I remember that." The windchill had been negative twenty degrees, a huge anomaly for a city whose temps never really went below zero. "I treated far too many animals for frostbite." Her shelter had also been overflowing with rescues. "The mayor made an announcement that any dogs and cats left outside would be confiscated and the owners cited for animal cruelty."

Suddenly it all fell together. That storm had been the catalyst for change, and by June, the mayor had formed the Animal Cruelty Task Force with its one officer—Jack. She watched as he ate another bite; as he popped a morsel in his mouth, hers dried. She struggled for composure. This was just lunch, not a date.

"Along with the rescue groups, I was out in that snow and those temps. I didn't go home for over forty-eight hours, maybe closer to seventy-two. I only slept an hour or two here or there. I would not make a good pet parent. I can't commit to providing attention. Work comes first."

She ripped open her package of thinly sliced cheddar and sour-cream flavored potato chips. "Still, I have cats and my neighbor—"

He reached for his water. "I can't ask a neighbor to care

for them. That's not fair to anyone." She watched as those beautiful lips took a long draught, his throat constricting as he swallowed. He set the bottle down and wiped his mouth, getting the drop that had caught the edge of his lip.

"What?" he asked.

"Nothing." She fibbed, hating that she'd been caught staring. Worse, like when someone yawned and someone repeated, she'd also swallowed. Hard. She grabbed her water and took a sip that failed to quench the heat she was feeling. Chemistry. Human magnetism. That's all this was. Nothing she couldn't squelch.

"You're really into Christmas, aren't you?"

His question caught her off guard, but it was a safe topic. "Love it. Can you tell?" Like the waiting room, she'd decorated here as well: a tiny Christmas tree on a table, some garland around the doorframe, and a porcelain Santa Claus collection on her desk. Fake poinsettias lined one wall. "Wouldn't you agree? Isn't it the best time of the year?"

Despite how cheery she'd made her office, he answered, "Debatable."

That wrinkle pinched the skin above her nose again, and she rubbed it with a finger. "Then how come you're Mr. December?"

He sighed. In a year, she'd be staring at him half naked for thirty-one days. Strange that thought didn't bother him as much as it should have. Maybe it was because he'd like to see her naked, her brown hair framed out on his white pillowcase. He'd never considered white lab coats sexy, but on Kat . . . he wondered what was underneath. He jolted to the present, focused on her question.

"They didn't ask us our favorite month. We just arrived and did what they told us to do."

"Oh." She seemed a little disappointed.

"Each of us got to pick where our portion of the proceeds went. As the task force is new and can use any publicity, and my lieutenant told me it would be good PR to do the calendar. I never considered all the consequences."

"Like?"

"Well, I'm the only cop permanently assigned to the task force, which means I'm the media darling. It's made me a bit of a target, and now that that calendar is out . . ."

Brown eyes reflected mischievousness tempered with a side of doubt. "Oh please. You mean to tell me you weren't flattered by all those women vying for your attention at the ball?"

"You mean my stalkers?"

"Fan club?"

"Stalkers. Or overzealous attention seekers? Calendar groupies? Those better terms?"

She had cheddar crumbs on her lips. He gestured, and she wiped with her forefinger. He clenched his hands, putting them safely in his lap before he did something stupid, like clean her lips with his tongue. "Surely the calendar fallout can't be that bad."

"Easy for you to say. I'm a blue-collar guy, and that shot turned me into a calendar stud. My work e-mail is public, and since the calendar debuted, the majority of my inbox is women asking me on dates. I had one or two file abuse claims, but those ended up being excuses to get me to stop by their residence—where at least two opened the door wearing nothing but smiles. It's hard to talk when looking at someone's feet."

"Sorry," Kat said, trying to contain her laughter.

"It's not funny," he argued.

"No, it's not," she agreed, shaking her head to stop from giggling. "But I'm picturing you trying to cover your eyes and—

"I have a year of this!"

She crumpled the chip in half and dropped it onto the white wrap paper of her sandwich. "I know. I'm being insensitive." She gave a wave, as if brushing off a fly. "Worse, you had to kiss me after that lady trapped us. Who knows what you thought when I said I wanted to be involved." She dissolved into laughter again. "No wonder why you ran away."

His expression was incredulous. "Away? You're the one who vanished. After the photo, you were gone. I looked for you."

She sat back in her chair with a hard thump, surprised. "You did?"

A cheeky grin made more butterflies take flight. "Heck, a man would be foolish not to go back after a kiss like that, and Kat, I'm no fool."

"Oh. Well." Frankly, she didn't know what to say. They were locked in a staring contest again, neither of them looking away.

"Kat?" Angela stood in the doorway. "Media is here again."

Saved by the bell. "We'll be out in a minute." She faced Jack. "I approached you because I wanted to help. Every pet deserves a good home. That's why I do this, spend so much time on my . . ."

"Shelter?" Jack filled in helpfully.

"Yes." She shouldn't be surprised he knew.

"That reminds me, I need to see your shelter. I have this letter."

The expression of hurt warped to anger. "Are you saying I'm not caring for Jingle?"

"No. I'm very impressed. You will continue to care for him."

Butterflies had been replaced with dread. She considered Jingle as her dog. She'd saved him. "What are your plans for Jingle?"

"Billy's heartbroken about his dog, but Jingle's not going back there, and I've convinced his parents he should not get another dog for a very long time."

That pacified her slightly. "Good idea."

"Besides, Jingle's evidence. When he's well and ready, Jeff at Pet Rescue will make sure he finds a good home."

"Jingle's not going to be ready for a while."

"Which is fine. But people are going to want to adopt him. He's something of a celebrity. They'll line up to adopt him. Remember Trooper, the dog pulled behind the car? Over a thousand people applied to be his new owner."

"I can find him a new owner when it's time."

"Let's see how your legal problems pan out. Jingle just brought me here earlier. You and I would have been meeting Monday anyway. I'm going to need to inspect you. I received a complaint."

Disbelief bubbled. She gestured to the food. "So this was all just to butter me up? You're toying with me?"

Jack shifted uncomfortably. "No. I . . ."

"Hey guys." This time Anthony poked his head in. "Sorry to interrupt. Busy schedule today."

"No problem. We are finished," Kat said. She willed her anger not to show as all the ease of lunch disappeared.

She and Jack went out into the waiting area, where the cameraman had everything set up. She put the mic on, this time by herself.

"So Dr. Saunders," Anthony asked. "How's Jingle?"

Kat went through the basics, including telling him that the front desk had already fielded calls from people wanting to adopt him. "We're keeping a list while trying to refer them to our other animals and other shelters," Kat said.

"People only want what they see on TV." Jack's cynicism came through loud and clear.

"You aren't going to run that, are you?" Kat asked.

"Not miked, and Anthony wouldn't do that," Jack replied.

Anthony shook his head. "Nah, people want a feel-good story. Like, Kat, my research showed you found homes for about two hundred animals over the last twelve months."

A sinking feeling formed in Kat's stomach. Jack listened avidly. "Yes. I screen every adopter myself."

Anthony tilted his head. "That's great. Two hundred animals?"

"Yes." She was proud of this accomplishment. "It's our best year yet and we still have our upcoming December adopt-a-thon. The holidays are such a great time for pet adoptions."

She saw Jack's frown. "What? You don't like those either?"

"I'm not a big fan of the over-commercialized Christmas industry, no. And I worry about people who give pets at Christmas. Do you know how many pet-store pets end up in shelters?"

Anthony's head pivoted back and forth.

"Well, I am much more successful. And surely you love Christmas. It's the best time of the year. The caroling. The parties. The visiting with old friends."

He didn't speak for a minute. "I don't hate it."

"Guys, we need to get back on track. I have a deadline."

Kat couldn't understand how anyone could have so little Christmas spirit. "Did you have a bad childhood experience? My cousin's husband's parents were divorced, so he got passed around from family to family, so until he had his own kids he wasn't a fan."

"My mom and stepdad have been married almost twenty years. Christmas Day we eat brunch at twelve thirty like we always do, although now we do a Rob Your Neighbor game. As for my dad, he's living in Tampa and has been for years. So, really it's nothing like what you mentioned."

"This has nothing to do with Jingle," Anthony interjected hopefully.

"Sorry," Kat replied, glad her waiting room was currently empty. "I just want to know the answer."

"It's complicated," Jack replied. "And really—"

"Try me," she suggested.

"Please," Anthony begged. "I'm on deadline."

"That man needs his story," Jack replied, evading Kat's need to know.

She shoved her hands into her pockets, obviously irritated. "Fine."

Jack watched as Kat began the interview, glad he'd been given a reprieve from explaining feelings that—to any lover of Christmas—made him seem freakish. He had good reasons, but like a chocolate-lover not understanding how anyone could choose vanilla, his choices were beyond a Christmas lover's comprehension.

"So could you tell us how rescuing Jingle might impact your legal troubles?" Anthony suddenly asked. "Do you think you'll lose the fight?"

As Kat sputtered, Jack winced. Since yesterday, he'd researched her legal issues thoroughly. Since no abuse had been cited in the original complaint, he hadn't been called in—the city saw this as first and foremost a zoning issue. The letter addressed directly to him had changed things.

"You're running a rescue shelter without the necessary occupancy permits," Anthony continued. "Can you comment on this?"

Kat fought to remain calm. "The clinic where Jingle is being treated has all the required licensure and permits. Jingle is getting the best care and at no cost to the city, as I am underwriting all expenses as part of my partnership with the Animal Cruelty Task Force. I consider it an honor to be Jingle's vet."

"But what about the neighbors who've complained? And some say they've seen your shelter and you have dogs covered in their own feces."

Anthony had clearly been reading the comments following the news article. Family members of the neighbors who'd filed the complaints had written most of the vitriol.

"Those claims are groundless and have no basis in fact," Kat bit out, willing her voice to remain neutral.

"So . . ." Anthony probed.

"My lawyer has told me not to comment."

"Maybe you should," Jack said, stepping forward.

She shot him an angry glance.

"Here you have Anthony, who always tells a fair story, giving you the chance to set the record straight. And I'm here, and after the letter I received, I wanted to see your shelter for myself." He held out a piece of paper.

She'd let her guard down. Her impulsivity had cost her again. "You want to close me down," she accused.

"No. I have not reached a conclusion. I'm a fair man."

"He is." Anthony reached for the paper, but Jack put it in his pocket. "If you have nothing to hide—"

"Fine," Kat cut in, desperate to regain control of a situation fast spiraling out from under her.

"So we can have a tour?" Anthony prodded.

"Might get people in the door to adopt," Jack added. "And put this complaint to rest." He waved the paper again.

"I have nothing to be ashamed of." Cornered, she glanced at her watch. "But I only have twenty minutes before my next patient."

Anthony, now that he had his exclusive, went to speak with his cameraman.

"I can't believe this." Kat turned her anger on Jack. "You set me up." She snatched the letter from his hand.

"I meant to ask you last night, but it was late. The only reason I didn't insist yesterday is that Jeff approved you and I trust him. Kat, you have the most high profile dog in the city. And if dogs are standing in their own waste, then I want to see it for myself."

That hurt. "Do you really believe that of me?"

He shook his head. "No. But put my mind at ease anyway."

Which meant he doubted. *So much for their earlier connection.*

"We ready?" Anthony nudged, returning.

Kat led them to another part of the clinic. "We have a series of luxury boarding suites." She pointed to a series of mini rooms. "Here people can board their dogs or cats and choose the level of playtime, amount of grooming, and whether they want remote video access via the web." They crossed into another portion of the building. "This area is for our stray guests."

Immediately behind the door, the noise of barking dogs became extremely loud. Kat had twenty indoor kennels, each separated by chain link. The facility looked like most other pet shelters, and Jack noted the floors and kennels were extremely clean. "This door leads outside and we let them run in the yard. We also do leash training and take them on walks." Kat opened the door to a side yard, which was more than adequate space. "The dogs are always supervised."

She led them back inside and downstairs to a basement with ten-foot-high ceilings. "This is our cat facility." A few cats lounged by themselves in large cages with plenty of space; others lived together in a community room. The lighting and ventilation were more than adequate.

"Jack?" Anthony asked. He shoved a handheld mic under Jack's nose.

"I don't see any animal abuse or any unhealthy animals or an unsanitary environment," Jack answered honestly.

"As the detective who's cited several puppy mills for their poor conditions, you'd know bad facilities when you saw them."

"Yes, I would. At this time, Dr. Saunders's facility exceeds the requirements for a shelter. As for her occupancy permits, that's not my department and I can't address it."

"But do you think she should be able to keep her shelter?"

"I am always an advocate of animal adoptions," Jack replied, skirting the question with diplomatic aplomb. He handed the mic back.

"Well, I appreciate this," Anthony said. "I'll let you know if I have questions."

Kat tossed the letter on her desk and dropped into her chair the moment the news crew left. Jack remained standing, and Crystal came to weave herself between his legs. She trembled. "What a mess. A complete mess."

"I didn't lie," Jack told her. "I never lie. If you'd had any animal in distress, I'd be back in five minutes to take them away and shut you down."

"I know." She glanced at her watch. Six minutes before her next client. She prided herself on being on time. "I screwed up and it's biting me. I forgot to get the permits. It started out as one stray dog that my vet tech found. Then once I remodeled the clinic, I had more space and someone else brought me another. Then another. Next thing you know, I'm running an unofficial shelter and I'm in violation of zoning, and now I'm embroiled in a mess and headed to court. You forcing that tour put me in an awkward spot."

"I read the *Post-Dispatch* article. You need to clear the air and the minds of the city. You need good PR. The story can do that. It will stop this," he said holding up the letter.

She chewed her lower lip. "What if Anthony's story makes everything worse? My lawyer said—"

"My brother's a lawyer. They're always saying something."

"Yes but—"

"Worse would be that we have to relocate Jingle to another vet." He let that hang out there and then said gently, "Kat, your heart was in the right place when you started your shelter. You do everything in your power to save animals, including sleeping at your clinic. Those animals looked well cared for. I said that on camera, and it's the truth. But know that I will not let anything blemish the task force."

"Then you might have made the wrong choice with me. Especially depending on the comments that get posted after the news broadcast."

He shrugged. "You never know. Could be nothing."

She put her head in her hands. "I wish you hadn't put me on the spot. If this ruins my chances for my adoption event, I don't know what I'll do. What if the city shuts that down too? How will I find my animals homes then?"

"Christmas adoptions are never a good idea. Just look at Jingle."

Her head shot up and her chest heaved. "You're wrong. Many loving families find homes at Christmas, and my animals deserve that chance. Pet Rescue is full, as are most no-kill shelters. I will not have my animals end up in a kill shelter. If this gets screwed up, you'll need to help me fix it." Her watch beeped. She could not keep her patients waiting. "I have to go."

"I'll stop by after closing. See how Jingle's doing. We

can talk then. Discuss any fallout."

Overwhelmed, she rose to her feet. "I don't know if that's a good idea. I can keep you up-to-date over the phone. You've already done more than enough, and I probably shouldn't speak to you again without talking to my lawyer." She remembered her manners. "Thank you for lunch."

Jack towered over her. He cupped her chin, and awareness burned through her. Determined and slightly irritated blue eyes locked onto hers. "We're not finished, Kat. Not by a long shot. I will see you after work."

Chapter Four

That afternoon, Kat kept busy with back-to-back patients. She performed several routine physicals, saw one dog who'd chewed up a sneaker, and treated a cat that had an infection and needed an antibiotic shot and a special diet. During her appointments she'd fought to keep her mind from churning. Worry frayed her nerves, and her lawyer's $250 phone call hadn't helped either. She'd just reiterated that Kat needed to keep a low profile.

Kat changed Jingle's dressings, checked his wounds for infection, and monitored his vitals. "So how was lunch with Mr. December?" Angela asked.

"Jack," Kat corrected. She and Angela had worked together for three years now, and Angela's brows lifted at the correction.

"That sounds pretty friendly."

Kat ran her fingers through her hair, a nervous habit. "We aren't friendly. He showed up here with a complaint letter. He came to investigate me, and the interview probably ruined my chances with the city."

"So, make him fix it. Have Jack help you with the adoption event. He said he's a fair guy. Make him prove it."

"What are you suggesting?"

Angela shrugged. "Louise and I talked. He's a local celebrity. A press magnet. People will come here just to meet him, and after they do, maybe they'll go home with a new pet."

"Doesn't that prove his point?" Kat asked. "That people are fickle?"

"Ignore his Scrooge tendencies. Demand he help. He can sign some autographs or whatever. We get more people here, then we get more animals adopted. Claire will have the photos ready Monday, and we can start the heavy-duty PR."

Kat's clinic posted cute pictures of adoptable animals on its web site, which always helped with finding pets new homes. They'd hang up flyers on the public supermarket boards and advertise via Facebook and Petfinder.com. "Even with all that we do, we need press. We need to capitalize on Jingle and Jack," Angela insisted.

"I'm not sure involving either of them is a good idea. Probably a conflict of interest. Jack's not really thrilled with his fame."

Although a few years younger than Kat, Angela suddenly sounded far wiser. "Who cares? He allowed Anthony to come in here, which put you in a bind. So he should help you out. What can it hurt to ask him?"

"He hates Christmastime adoptions. He's going to say

no. And the city can and perhaps will shut down my event saying it's also unsanctioned."

"Which is why you need the press to love you. You need to be Jingle's angel. Heck, be all stray animals' guardian angel. Let's keep reinforcing that every time Anthony comes."

"Sounds mercenary."

"Kat, this is your life's passion. Your shelter. Your animals. What do we have to lose? Use Jack Donovan."

"I don't use people." That was unthinkable.

"Kat, I love you like a big sister. You're more than my boss. But you need to put on some boxing gloves and get into the ring. Trust me. Jack is your golden ticket."

That logic made sense, Kat thought. It didn't mean she liked it.

"Kat?" Louise, the front-desk receptionist, stood in the doorway.

"Yes?"

"Mr. Simons is here with Pebbles."

It was five minutes until closing, which meant it was an emergency. "What's wrong?"

"Shallow breathing. He says she's lying around. Won't eat or drink. Been that way for a day or two."

"Get her into room two."

Kat met Jasper Simons in room two, where Pebbles, a sixteen-year-old cat, lay on the table. Mr. Simons was in his mid-fifties and lived nearby. "I just thought she wasn't hungry the past few days, so I tried some new food and . . ."

"She's old, Jas," Kat said, placing her hand on Pebbles. She felt around, noting the cat's glassy eyes and shallow inhalations. "Sometimes these things come on very quickly."

"She's not going to make it, is she?" he asked.

Kat did a quick examination. She'd been treating Pebbles for five years and knew her well. "She's had a long life. A great one. I know you love her very much, but this is renal failure. We could do dialysis, but . . ."

His hand trembled. "So it's time?"

She delivered the news she so hated. "Yes. I think that would be best. And you know I would tell you if there was anything I could do. But it's time."

Grown men do cry, and Mr. Simons wiped away a tear. "Can I stay? Hold her? I don't want her to be alone."

Kat nodded. "Yes. She'd like that. I'll go get things ready and give you some privacy to say your goodbyes."

"Mr. December's here," Angela warned as Kat unlocked a medicine cabinet.

"He's going to have to wait," Kat replied, retrieving the vials she needed. She returned to the room, Mr. Simons's tears causing her to bite back her own. Pet owners had to see her as competent. Strong, yet sympathetic. Professional. She shaved off a small area of Pebble's fur and then administered the sedative. After the second medication, Pebbles slipped away quickly.

"Thank you." Mr. Simons stroked Pebble's still body. Fresh tears began. "That was peaceful."

Angela gently wrapped the animal in a blanket and

took her from the room. "I'm sorry for your loss," Kat said.

"What will Bam Bam do?" He mentioned his other cat.

"Later, when things have settled down, you and I can talk about whether Bam Bam needs a playmate," she said. "I'll help you. But right now Bam Bam will need your full attention and love. He'll be grieving too."

Louise entered, and Mr. Simons followed her from the room. Kat undid her ponytail, scratched the top of her head, and then secured the strands again. She went to check on Jingle, and heard Jack. He cooed to the puppy in that baby talk that all animal lovers use, but that no one ever admits to. She watched him stroke the dog's head, his fingers gentle and soothing. He whispered in Jingle's ear. While Jingle's right ear twitched slightly, his eyes remained closed. Yet the dog seemed more peaceful.

"You sweet thing. I'm gonna get them for you. And you'll never hurt again. I promise." He glanced up, sensing her presence. He reddened, caught. Who'd have predicted Mr. Rough and Tough had such a soft side?

Softening, she said, "I'm sure he likes you talking to him."

"How's he doing?" He'd changed from his jeans and flannel shirt and now wore a pair of khakis and a blue oxford button-down that complimented his eyes.

Kat placed a hand on the dog's front right paw, one of the few areas that hadn't been burned. She touched Jingle as often as possible, letting him know she cared. "He's the same. We're keeping him sedated. The pain from the burns is unbearable. Later he'll need laser therapy and skin grafts, but we can't do those yet."

"But he's okay."

"We're constantly fighting off infection, so I can't rule anything out, but I am cautiously optimistic. His progress is promising."

"Good. I need updated pictures." He held out a small camera.

Kat was exhausted. She wanted to be alone, grieve for her role in the circle of life. "Tonight is not a good time."

He sensed that something was bothering her. "Then when can I get those?"

"How about Monday morning at eight? We'll be changing the bandages, so that will be a good time."

"I'll be here for that," Jack said, putting the camera in his jacket pocket. "That's fine. The more evidence we can present to the jury of this dog's suffering, the better chance we have for a conviction. It's not only about demonstrating the horror of the act itself, but of the recovery this poor dog also has suffered."

Kat tucked a loose strand behind her ear. "Do you know who did it?"

One simple nod. "Yes."

After the day she'd had, she needed to know. "Who?"

"The boy's aunt and her boyfriend."

Kat's hand flew up in front of her mouth as she gasped. "Billy's relatives? His own family?"

"Yes. Jingle bit the aunt's son, and she decided to punish the dog by ending his life. She bragged on Facebook, saying all dogs don't go to heaven and 'smell that doggie smoke.'"

"You have to be kidding me. That's sick." Kat's whole body shook from the horrible revelation.

"Sick's an understatement. I'll be arresting her and her boyfriend within days. We only need a few more digital footprint pieces on the boyfriend, and we'll pick them both up. I want rock-solid arrests. I want convictions."

Kat did too. She rubbed Jingle's paw, her touch gentle. Mr. Simons had loved Pebbles more than anything, and he'd gone home heartbroken. The people who'd hurt Jingle were the worst kind on earth. Kat's fury raged and her body shook.

"Hey, what's wrong?"

The day overwhelmed. "I just had to put a cat down and watch his owner unravel. This poor defenseless baby. Sweet Jingle. How could she do such a thing. . . . I . . . I . . . I'd . . ."

Kat shuddered as well-controlled emotions broke through the dam. A tear dropped and then another, and she furiously wiped them away.

"Hey." Jack folded her into his arms, and she went without hesitation. Cocooned, as if she belonged. "Yeah, I'd like to kill her too. But since that's not an option, I'm going to personally arrest her and her boyfriend and make sure it's the day's top news story. She's going to do hard time if I have anything to say about it. They both are."

Kat sniffled, tried to stem the flow. "Justice is slow."

"We're building an airtight case. They won't get away with this."

"I hope so. For Jingle's sake." Kat stepped out of Jack's embrace. She'd liked being in his arms a little too much. "I have to check on the kennels."

"Can I tag along?"

Drained, Kat simply nodded. She didn't want to argue anymore. Jack followed as she went to visit both the stray animals and those being boarded. He helped her pet the excited dogs, scratched the heads of the purring cats. He had a magical touch. Cats rubbed against him, dogs quieted as he scratched behind their ears.

"I am really sorry about the cat."

His tenderness struck the right cord. "Me too. It's a part of life, but it's heartbreaking."

They greeted a few more of her animals. "I'm sorry about how we left things today. That was not my intention. I wasn't trying to ambush you. You're different from most women I've met. In a good way."

He couldn't put his finger on how, or why, but like the detective he was, knew he couldn't stop until he'd figured out the mystery. She didn't answer, just absorbed his words as she went to the next cat cage.

"So who's this?" he asked, and he trailed her, enjoying her company as she gave him some background on each animal. He wasn't in any real rush. She was his sole focus.

"Are you sleeping here again?"

"Yes. My partner says he'll stay tomorrow night. We have couches in our offices for just such purposes and with Jingle's condition, in case anything happens, I don't want to leave him alone too long. There is a staff member here, even on Sundays."

"You run a first-rate operation. You are impressive, Kat. I've never met someone as dedicated as you."

He smiled, and his compliment warmed her heart. He reached out and touched her arm, and the simple movement stirring a dormant fire, a fire she needed to squelch lest she get burned. "Now that I am a partner, we shouldn't let things get muddled, especially as you are investigating me."

"I responded to the complaint and dismissed it. It's clear there's no abuse."

"Still, I'm not sure if it's best that we blur professional lines."

He leaned against a table, assessed her with those all-seeing eyes. "Do you always do what's best?"

"Clearly not as I'm running a shelter with no permits." She sighed and scratched the head of a two-year-old tabby.

Angela poked her head around the corner. "There you are."

Kat jerked her finger out of the cage and put a startled hand on her chest. "You're still here?"

"I wanted to make sure Pebbles was ready for her cremation. And I wrote the sympathy card and put it in the mail."

The clinic had a policy of sending cards. It was the least they could do. "That's sweet of you for taking on that job for me."

"No problem. You can reward me with a big Christmas bonus. Did she eat?" This question was directed at Jack.

"Not that I know of."

Angela gave Kat a pointed look. "Lunch was hours

ago." As proof, Kat's stomach rumbled. "See?"

Caught, Kat gave a weak chuckle. However, it cut the tension and lightened her mood. "I am hungry."

"You need to eat. Let me take you somewhere," Jack inserted.

Angela beamed. "Great idea. I'll hold down the fort until you get back. You need to get out of here for a while. Besides, you have remote access."

"I can monitor Jingle's machines and watch him via my phone," Kat explained. "I do need to stop by my house and feed my cats."

"So go," Angela urged. She made a shooing motion and shot Kat a pointed look. "Go hug your kitties so you'll feel better. I'll be here."

She hesitated. "If you're sure . . ."

Angela practically pushed Kat out the door. "Go. I got this. And remember what I told you earlier."

"What did she tell you earlier?" Jack asked.

"Nothing important," Kat fibbed, allowing Jack to lead her toward an exit. She followed behind, noting his broad backside and the way his blond hair curled at the nape. She had an urge to touch those strands.

He assisted her into the SUV, her hand warming under his touch as he propelled her upward. He climbed into the driver's seat and leaned over to touch the clasp. "Buckled up?"

She nodded, wanting to trust him. But trust had failed her before. "Yes."

"Then let's do this."

Chapter Five

Ten minutes later Jack easily found Kat's apartment, for when she'd said the one with the Christmas lights, she hadn't been joking. The brick two-family building across from the park was completely covered. Blinking multicolored strands hung from the flat roofline and lined each window and door. She had a set of lighted white reindeer and one of those inflatable Santa Claus figures in the postage-stamp-size front yard.

While the neighboring buildings on each side also sported strands of lights, Kat's outshone both.

He parked in the alley, behind her two-car garage, and followed her through the well-lit yard to the back door. Christmas lights adorned the backyard trees as well as the garage.

"You in a contest?" he asked.

She laughed, put the key in the back-door lock. "No, but I just love the lights and decorations; it makes even a bad day like today a little brighter this time of year. I can hang more decorations here than at the clinic, so I admittedly go a bit overboard. I love that people slow down when they drive by."

She tugged the door open and turned off the first alarm as they stepped onto a small landing. Stairs led downstairs to the basement and also upward. "I'm on the second floor."

They passed the door to the first-floor apartment, and Jack tried not to stare too hard at her backside. "So do your tenants like all the lights?"

"Well, they don't mind, and their kids always tell me how much they love them. You?"

"I don't mind looking at Christmas lights," Jack replied as they climbed the stairs. She had a shapely backside—temptation was mere inches away. All he had to do was reach up. . . . Instead he shoved his hands deeper into his jacket pockets as they reached the second-floor landing.

He noted with a cop's satisfaction that she had a second alarm that went off when they stepped into her kitchen. While she made quick work of the code, he assessed the area, committing to memory the Santa aprons hanging on pegs in her kitchen. "This way."

In her living room, an ornament-covered live tree stopped inches short of the nine-foot ceiling. Upon their approach, a Siamese cat rose to its feet, arched its back and blinked. Then it stretched and sat on the edge of the couch. "That's Ty. He's a sweetheart. Pippa's around here somewhere, probably under the tree if she's not up in it.

Make yourself at home. I'll only be a minute."

Jack approached Ty, who clearly waited for a head scratch. Jack's phone buzzed; he grimaced at the caller ID. "Hi Mom."

"Jack. Saw you on the news a few minutes ago. How's that poor puppy?"

"Doing much better."

"That's good. Good. Did you get my e-mail?"

He had, and promptly ignored it.

"We need to know if you're bringing a date to your sister's wedding," his mother insisted. "If not, I have a solution."

Jack's fingers tightened on his cell. "I'm in the middle of something. Can I call you tomorrow?"

"Will you actually call me?"

She knew him well. He didn't/couldn't forget—but he'd just get busy and hours would pass. "I'll call the moment you get home from church. Still around noon?"

"Yes. Cecily and Brian are coming over at four and staying through dinner. We have a few more wedding details to finalize. You could stop by, you know. She'd love to see you. Why don't you come? We've missed you lately. You could watch football with your father. The Rams are playing the Saints. Starts at three."

While he loved his stepsister, who'd been four when she'd become part of his family, the last thing he wanted was to listen to his mother and Cecily ramble on about the nuptials occurring in three weeks. He'd already been fitted for a tux. Now they were hounding him for his plus one.

"I'm working tomorrow," he told his mother, which wasn't exactly a lie. He was always working.

"If you could try . . ."

"I might be able make it around six," he conceded.

"We'll be eating by then and trimming the tree afterwards."

Which meant he'd be conned into helping his mother turn her house into an overboard winter wonderland. "I'll see what I can do. But I will call you no matter what."

"You better. We're finishing the seating chart tomorrow, and I must have your answer by four thirty or I'm putting you next to Jane Moorhead. You remember Jane, right? She's flying in from Stanford where she's studying to be a lawyer. Pretty thing. Really blossomed from that girl you threw mud at in third grade. Could be the one for you. God knows Julie wasn't."

Jack grew impatient. "Mom, you loved Julie up until she dumped me, and I really do have to go," he said, for glittery round red ornaments were cascading from the Christmas tree and thudding onto the floor. He'd found Pippa, the longhaired calico kitten currently shaking the branches and testing the theory of gravity. "Love you!" he told his mom as he ended the call. He shoved his cell phone in his pocket and made a fast grab for the next ornament.

"They're not glass," Kat said behind him.

"Didn't think so but . . ." He tossed her the satin ornament, and she caught it one-handed and set it in a bowl on the dining room table.

"It's a game. Pippa knocks everything off the low

branches, so cloth ornaments only for the first four feet. The breakable things are up at the top where she can't get them. She also tries to pull the tinsel off, but she won't eat it, so it's safe. It just drapes badly at the floor."

He lifted a fallen strand of silver and looped it back over a low branch. "I can see that. You ready?"

Pippa launched a few more balls, before flying out of the tree to scramble after one. Her tiny paws flew out from under her, and she went sliding sideways on the hardwood before she tackled her prey. Then she jumped a foot skyward.

Jack and Kat looked at each other and laughed. "I'm ready. Food and water are filled." She gave Ty a scratch on the head. "You'll see me in the morning, won't you sweetie?" Ty flicked his tail and headed for the kitchen. He crunched on kibble as Kat locked up.

"Pizza okay?" Jack asked. "I was thinking Louie's, as it's close to the clinic."

"Love that place. Another good choice. You know your restaurants."

"I like good food," Jack said.

He patted his stomach and her mouth watered. No extra pounds there. When she'd been in his arms, she'd touched solid muscle, with not an ounce of flab. Against his chest during their hugs, she'd heard the powerful *thump thump* beneath his shirt. Her hands itched to touch his chest, feel the texture of his smooth skin. He was heavenly. Divine. Her body remained on high alert as they walked downstairs.

He assisted her both into and out of the SUV, his touch lingering as they reached Louie's. The place wasn't much to look at from the outside, but the plate glass window revealed a line of people waiting for carryout orders. They sat toward the back at the last empty table, and their waitress came for their drink order.

"After today, a glass of wine is in order," Kat said, ordering a Riesling. Jack opted for a Budweiser. The waitress wrote it down on her green pad and disappeared, but not before giving Jack an odd look.

"Do you think she recognizes you?"

"My family is pretty big. We know everyone it seems. It's like a very small world. You?"

"Only child," Kat admitted. "My parents were always busy with their medical professions, and I actually had a nanny. My dad traveled a lot and my mother worked long hours."

He arched a sexy blond brow. "Really?"

She nodded.

"Wow. My mother was always home and in everyone's business. Still is." He tapped his fingers on the table, then stilled the nervous habit. The waitress returned with their drinks, and he wrapped his fingers around the cold bottle and lifted it.

"Cheers," he said.

Kat's forehead creased quizzically. "To what? It's not been that good of a day. Rather lousy actually."

"Then how about we toast to Jingle, who's made it this far. That's reason to cheer."

"Fair enough." She perked up and clinked her wineglass to his bottle. Each took a sip.

"Speaking of Jingle, I watched the new story. Anthony did a nice job. You were portrayed in a positive light, so that should help with your legal troubles."

Kat unrolled her flatware. "I saw it, and I hope so. My lawyer called. She wasn't too pleased with the interview."

"Lawyers are a pain. Necessary evil."

"So you said you're brother is a lawyer."

"Yeah, when we were little I said I'd catch them and he'd put them away. One of the few times we agreed. But he went into corporate litigation. Pays better."

Kat sensed there was more, but didn't want to press. "What made you want to be a police officer?"

"I liked all those Encyclopedia Brown and Hardy Boys books. Then I moved to mysteries as I got older, working my way through Agatha Christie, all the Sherlock Holmes. He observed everything, and I have a memory that allowed me to do that too. I like problem solving. I also liked Dick Francis."

"I've read a few of his. He was a jockey. Did race horse mysteries."

"Yeah. Once I chose the police force, I thought it'd be cool to be a member of St. Louis's mounted police. Instead, I realized that I could do more good by helping animals rather than riding them. I get to do more detective work this way. And I can't stand to see innocent creatures suffer."

"Sounds noble."

He shrugged, clearly reluctant to accept praise. "No

more than saving animals like you do."

The young waitress returned and held out a copy of the calendar. "Are you Jack Donovan?"

He gave her the media smile. "I am."

"Could you autograph this? We're going to be hanging it in back come January. How cool that you eat here. Well, you will once I get your order." Unlike Kat's laugh, the waitress's light giggle got on Jack's nerves.

He signed the calendar with a flourish, and then they ordered a St. Louis–style, thin-crust green pepper and onion pizza. Kat added an Italian salad for a starter.

"Does that happen often?" Kat asked after the waitress departed. Now other patrons were looking at them and pointing and whispering.

"More and more," he admitted. "It's a bit unnerving."

Kat heard snatches of "vet" and "Jingle." Surprise had her eyes widening. "They're talking about me."

Jack shrugged. "It's nothing. Ignore it. You have to or it'll drive you crazy."

She tried, but after a few minutes said, "You're right. It's annoying. How do you put up with it?"

"It's part of the job."

Kat sighed. Then her ears perked up. "Now they're talking about my legal issues."

"Ignore them."

She hated being the subject of gossip. "I can't. I'm so worried. It should have been a simple permit fix. It's blown up into this huge issue. Do you know how much money I invested? My parents told me it was a waste. But I don't like animals to suffer any more than you do. All I wanted to do was help."

"I'm truly sorry." He sipped his beer, mouth wrapping around the opening. "It has to be hard."

He swallowed, the mesmerizing sight momentarily stripping her of her focus. A routine act shouldn't be so darn sexy. What had she been about to say? Oh yeah. She blinked. "It hasn't been an easy process."

He reached for her hand, covered it with his. "What can I do?"

"I was hoping, wondering—" She stopped. She couldn't do this. She pulled her hand away, breaking the magnetic connection, and he let her fingers go.

"I want to help," he prodded.

Kat clenched her hands in her lap, twisted them together. "I can't. Even though I got put on the spot, I'm now as bad as all those other women who wanted something from you, or I'll sound like an autograph-seeking fangirl like our waitress."

"Try me."

She released her hands and sipped her wine for courage. "You know I've a huge adoption event coming up. We hope to clear out the shelter, which we need to do just in case things don't go my way in court . . ."

Her voice trailed off and she took a deep, fortifying breath. "I'd like you to be our celebrity guest. You'd talk to people, help them choose an animal, sign some autographs . . . maybe even wear a Santa hat."

He didn't respond, and she placed both hands flat on

the table and sighed. "I know. Poor joke. Plus, It's everything you hate, but you might be my last hope. I honestly don't know what else to do. I was impulsive and once again it bit me."

The waiter set her salad down, then topped off their water glasses. Jack lifted his beer to his lips, let a good long sip pass. Then he set the brew down and brushed some lint off the red and white plastic tablecloth. "I told you how I feel about animals being Christmas presents; they are a huge responsibility. Jingle was a present."

She bristled. "I screen every adopter personally. I'm like an animal-human love connection. I also have a return policy. If they don't want the animal, no matter when, they are to bring it back to me."

"Even if you don't have a shelter?"

She jutted her chin forward. "I will work something out."

He toyed with the frosted red plastic water glass, wiping away a bead of condensation. "How many come back?"

"We've had a few," she admitted, "but not as many as you'd expect. Less than two percent. And I've been able to find new homes for each one. All of my dog owners can partake in free obedience classes held here at my clinic. While you may not like Christmas, it's a great time to get a pet because people are home. Kids are off school for at least a week, so there are people around during the day to assimilate the animal. I also hold kiddie classes to teach children proper pet care. Good animal care comes from education. Kids need to learn how to show appropriate affection and how to take care of their pets. I provide that."

His fingers moved up and down the bottle in an absent caress. If those fingers were on her . . . Her mouth dried and she took a long, nourishing sip of cold wine. "Seems like you've thought of everything."

She nodded, and her loose brown hair swished around her neck and brushed the tops of her shoulders. "I've made my clinic full service. I do not want what happened to Jingle happening to any of my animals."

He liked how she said "my animals." Saving pets was a calling, not just a mission, not just a job. On that point, at least, they were kindred spirits. "What if we did it at a later time?" he asked.

She finished her Riesling. "You're missing my point. I know you hate Christmas adoptions, but I am out of time. My hearing is right before the holiday. I have mere weeks to find homes for twenty dogs and fourteen cats. I'll do anything to save them. Anything."

That caught his interest. "Anything?"

"Anything." That had come out wrong. "Well, within reason." Where was that waitress? More wine. Stat.

Those fingers continued their sensual assault on the cup. "So, if I do you this favor, will you owe me one?"

"What?"

"Owe me one." He repeated, those three words subtly suggestive. Kat's breath hitched. *Just what did he mean?* He rubbed his fingers together then reached for the beer bottle. "If I do this, I want quid pro quo."

She'd grabbed her fork, then set it back down. Was he really considering helping her? "Like what?"

"You want to use me, yes? My particular skills?" The words rolled seductively off his tongue, sending an anticipatory shiver to her toes. She could think of all kinds of skills she'd like to use, none involving signing calendars or finding homes.

Oh boy. Her impulsivity once again had her in far too deep. His lips molded around the bottle opening. Her mouth dried, and she sipped water for much needed composure. "I sound like all those women. It was Angela's idea. Forget I asked."

"I never forget a thing."

"No?"

"No. It's one of the reasons I became a cop. It's also the reason that kiss we shared is so potent. Or that I wouldn't like to try it again."

"Oh." She let that sink in.

"First, I am not posing sans clothes . . . in public."

Her skin heated and she blushed deep. "I wouldn't expect that."

Beer slid down his throat. "You'd be amazed who would and how many times I've been asked." Bottle down, long, firm fingers now tapped against the plastic water cup. "Also, I'm happy to take pictures and sign autographs, but I don't want that to be my only focus. As much as I hate Christmastime adoptions, I do like helping people find a pet. I also want to be able to publicize the Task Force and its work. So we need to make sure all animals are going to good, forever homes."

She nodded, hopeful. "Of course. You know I support all of that."

"Finally, I have another condition. A personal favor, so to speak."

As the idea germinated, he realized he'd found the perfect solution to his number-one problem. He could get his mother off his back and explore this thing—this interest—he had with Kat.

"Like what kind of favor?" she asked.

"I need you to fall madly in love with me."

Her fingers flew to her mouth. "What?"

He laughed, put his hands up in surrender. "Kidding. But have you ever seen one of those movies where people agree to help each other out during the holidays? You know, like attending events together? But as friends? But they pretend to be dating? I need us to do that."

She tugged her bottom lip under with her top teeth. "Let me get this straight. Are you talking about Hallmark Channel Christmas movies? And you want us to pretend to be in love?"

A shoulder lifted in a shrug. "Yes and yes."

"You watch Hallmark movies?"

"My mother and sister do. And"—he turned it around on her—"I bet you've probably seen every one."

Busted. "Okay, fine." The rosy flush spread, and his breath caught. "Yes, I watch them marathon style. Don't you dare snicker. There's nothing wrong with that. Don't knock me or your mother for our good taste."

"Or my stepsister," he added, grateful he and Kat had connected. "She's getting married in a few weeks. Which is why I need you to pretend to be mad about me. Remember my stalkers from the ball? My mom's fault. She's a self-proclaimed matchmaker and determined to fix me up. I need a buffer, like you were the night we met. You love Christmas and December, so you're perfect."

"I'm far from perfect."

"Not for this." Intense blue eyes stopped studying the cup, locking onto her gaze instead. A shiver ran through her. "If I do your charity event, I want you to attend some events with me."

That sounded doable. "Why?"

"I need to get through this holiday and could use publicity for the unit. With a beautiful, intelligent woman on my arm, I will be left alone. If we fake date, it's a win-win."

Her eyes widened, comprehending. "You need a mercy date."

"And you need me to help save your shelter."

"Sounds like we're both desperate."

"I am never desperate."

Kat trembled at the innuendo. No, a man as sexy as him wouldn't be. He shook his head, that blond hair dropping into his face. Then he let out a long sigh. "But I do need us to pretend we're a newly in-love couple. Only you and I will know it's all make-believe. Can you do that?"

Her lips puckered together. Could she pretend to be in love with him—the sexiest guy to come along in years?

Kat studied her untouched salad as if the croutons had grown wings. Just this morning he'd waved a complaint letter in her face. "It's a lot to take in." Grabbing her fork, she stabbed a chunk of lettuce and cheese. The idea of spending more time with him sent chills up her body. As she used her napkin to wipe her lips, she recalled the sensation of their kiss. She pulled her fingers away. *It's for the animals,* she scolded herself. "So what events?"

He visibly relaxed. "Mainly my stepsister's wedding and all the family stuff surrounding it. And the Pet Rescue Ball. If it's anything like the calendar ball, I want a wingman to run interference." He shuddered, the memory clearly disturbing.

"There are a few other things too, but we can discuss those later. Anyway, I'll help you with your shelter and your legal things, if you keep my meddling mother and every other women who sees me as an eligible boy toy at bay."

"So I'm to be your girlfriend." She rolled the word over her tongue, trying it out.

"To everyone else, yes. Only we'll know the truth. You've already seen me in a tux and as we've already shared a kiss, it shouldn't be too awkward to pretend to like me or share a few more kisses, right?"

"I . . . uh . . ." One kiss had been earthshaking.

He bulldozed ahead. "I'll tell my mother plus one when I call her tomorrow. That is, if we have a deal. Do we? Are you in?"

Once again, like with the tour, he'd put her between a

rock and a hard place. But she needed help. She needed a miracle to save her shelter. Jack, Mr. Animal Task Force, could be exactly what she needed.

"Before I say yes . . ." Kat began.

"Ask away."

"You're a smart, intelligent and, honestly, a hot guy."

"Hot huh?"

"I'm sure your stalkers have massaged your ego enough. So why me?"

"Because I like you." Words every woman wanted to hear, until they were followed with, "But I'm not looking for happily ever after. My job comes first. If my mother understood that, I wouldn't be in this situation. She's already got my wedding date set. A Jane Moorhead. Went to Stanford."

Kat ate more pizza as each fell to his and her thoughts. Finally Kat spoke. "You do realize that in all those Hallmark movies the fake couple always falls in love."

Jack didn't appear too concerned. "Ah, the magic of Hollywood." He tilted his head, that blue-eyed gaze intense as he studied her. "You certainly have the beauty part down."

A zing ricocheted through her "You think I'm beautiful?"

"Of course you are." He seemed amused by her surprise. "My family will love you."

The real reason for the farce. Which was a shame. For she found Jack very attractive as well. Liked how his lips felt on hers. Wondered how much his touch might ignite.

But cold-bloodedly discussing fake dating with Mr. Hot and Sexy, albeit with flirting, just proved that once again she'd found Mr. Wrong. The thought made her a little sad, and she brushed it aside.

"I'd like us to be friends," Jack confirmed. "We can make that happen if we go into this arrangement with our eyes open. I like you. It's a simple transaction. I help you and you keep my family off my back."

"For how long?"

He looked up, as if the stucco ceiling would have the answer. "How about until right after New Year's? We'll be seeing each other that long anyway because of Jingle. Even thought our contact will continue, New Year's Eve should do it."

December 31. The one holiday she hated. With all her friends married, Kat was always odd man out. She put another piece of pizza on her plate but made no move to take a bite. She wiped her hand on a napkin. "So, would you be willing to attend things with me? If I needed you?"

Jack tilted his head, considered. "Why not? My mom would think it strange if I didn't."

Kat assessed one of the most beautiful men she'd ever seen. As long as she kept her emotions in check, she could revive Jack's missing Christmas spirit and get through the holidays without being the odd singleton everyone felt sorry for. At twenty-eight, she was as tired of those helpfully nosy and well-intentioned conversations as Jack seemed to be. Since he was clearly a workaholic and since Kat had had enough of coming in second to last a lifetime, she should be safe. And her animals would be taken care of.

She stretched her hand, the zing as she touched Jack's fingers a clear warning of blatant chemistry that she chose to ignore. She would be the Jack Donovan's perfect fake girlfriend to save her animals. She could even kiss him a few times if necessary. That would certainly be no hardship. Butterflies danced in her stomach. Nope. No difficulty whatsoever. The man turned her on, sent tingles to her toes. All she had to do was stay in control, keep all rampant desire in check and her heart protected. Easy, right?

"Jack Donovan," she said, shaking his hand, grip firm as heat fused their fingers together, "you have yourself a deal."

Chapter Six

"You have a date. Really? A date?"

"Geez," Jack said, realizing that perhaps choosing to drop his bombshell while his mother was whipping mashed potatoes with a hand mixer hadn't been the best idea. The bowl slid forward, and as she grabbed for it, white fluffy blobs arched into the air, hitting the wall and floor as the beaters lost their traction.

"I'll get it," Jack said, grabbing for the roll of paper towels.

His mom powered off the mixer, leaving it perched against the edge of the bowl. She held out her hand. "Give them to me."

Jack counted off three sheets of the quicker picker upper and passed them over. He leaned against the counter and stuck the rest back onto the holder.

"What's with the mess?" Jack's stepdad asked, squeezing into the small space.

"Jack has a date!" his mother announced.

"Really?"

"Yes," Jack finished, as Nelson opened the refrigerator door and grabbed two more beers.

"Two?" his mom asked, arms crossed.

Nelson held a bottle up. "One's for Brian. Cecily's bombarding him with another wedding decision. This way he can pretend his eyes are glazing over from an alcoholic haze. Luckily halftime's about to end."

There was a long-standing, unwritten rule in the household that only football talk was allowed during the Rams game.

"Poor dear. He's earned it. He's been a good sport. Your sister has been a little outlandish at times."

Jack figured that was an understatement. His mom wiped her hands on her apron. "Well, tell Cecily that Jack has his plus one. He's bringing a date."

Jack's stepdad gave him a once-over. "Thank God. Now Cecily can stop harping over her seating chart and get it done. You want a beer?"

Jack held up his bottle. "I'm good."

His mother added a half stick of butter to the potatoes and started the mixer. "If you're not helping, get out of the kitchen."

His stepdad gave Jack a wink and parted with, "I help by getting out of the way. And halftime's over."

"He's actually been great about the wedding," his mom said when Nelson left, beating the softened butter into submission. "So who is she?"

"Who is who?" Cecily asked as she came through the

dining room door. "Game's back on. I've been banished."

"The who is Jack's date. He's actually bringing someone to your wedding."

"Really?" Cecily's eyes narrowed. "She's not from one eight hundred rent-a-babe is she?"

"Ha-ha. I can date, you know," Jack said, irritated that she'd practically snorted her disbelief. "I have a date and she's real."

"So this isn't just a ploy to get out of it and then show up by yourself? I mean, you do know who's going to be there."

"I do not want to sit by Jane Moorhead."

"I meant—" Cecily began, but Jack cut her off.

"I have a date." Jack gritted his teeth. "Put me down for plus one and let's drop it."

"Wow. Mr. I'm Too Busy for Women has a real date," Cecily said. She took her phone out of her pocket. "I'm making a note of this now. What's her name?"

"Kat."

"You're bringing a cat to my wedding?"

From the moment he'd first met Cecily, she'd always made it her unmerciful mission to get on his last nerves. Eight years younger, she'd been in her terrible twos when her dad had married Jack's mom. Of course, Jack loved her dearly and wouldn't trade her for the world.

"Her name is Katherine," Jack gritted out, his memory recalling the bright blue stitching right above Kat's heart. Her lab coat had done little to hide her figure and . . . He replaced that memory with the dress she'd worn to the calendar ball—then gave himself a mental cold shower.

"Do we know her? And K? Or C? Or . . ."

"K-A-T-H-E-R-I-N-E," he spelled as his sister typed the note into her phone. "Saunders. S-A-U-N-D-E-R-S. She's a vet."

"A vet. Sounds kind of perfect, with you working with animals," Cecily said.

"She's at the Chippewa Animal Clinic."

"Oh! The one who saved Jingle!" his mother said over the mixer noise, the potatoes almost to whipped perfection. "She was very pretty on TV."

Close enough. He could always correct the story later if need be. "Well, one thing led to the next and I asked her out. We're going to the Pet Rescue gala and then I thought, why not the wedding? Especially with both of you harping on me."

"All the single ladies will be so disappointed," his mother said. "But I'm sure Jane Moorhead will somehow survive."

Cecily nodded. "True, and it's not like Brian doesn't have a lot of single friends. We are the first ones to get married out of our group of friends."

"Too young if you ask me," Jack said.

Her forehead creased into a scowl. "Really Jack, I am tired of your negativity. I'm twenty-two, I finished college, I'm working, and I love Brian. Why can't I get married? Just because you can't find a woman with whom to close the deal doesn't mean I don't know what I am doing."

"So how do you know he's the right one?" That

question had been what had held Jack back—why he'd never asked Julie to marry him. Somehow he'd been uncertain, his gut telling him "no."

"I knew that I would marry him back when I was six and punched him in the nose after he said that girls have cooties. I just knew. And even though we dated other people during our freshman year of college, it's always been him."

"Fair enough. Good enough for me." Jack extricated himself from the conversation by pulling Cecily into his arms for a bone-crushing hug. Her phone pressed against his chest. "I only want my little sister to be happy. And I'd hate to have to shoot him on your behalf."

"Oh, he knows what he's getting into. He's always known, and I love him because he's not intimidated by my family." Cecily paused, then laughed. "Well, maybe a little. Dad's in there plying him with beer and football, and Brian's letting him all in the name of bonding with his soon-to-be father-in-law. Looks like *I'll* be driving home."

"Dinner's ready," Jack's mom announced. "And Nelson," she called into the other room, "you better hit that pause button on the DVR. You can watch when we're finished and skip through the commercials. You will give this family at least forty-five minutes of your time."

"Yes dear," came the reply, for while no one better talk during Nelson's Sunday football, the flipside was that for the past twenty years Sunday dinner had gone on the table promptly at five thirty, football be darned. Needless to say, Jack's stepdad had been the first one on his block to own and master the use of a DVR.

Jack and Cecily grabbed serving dishes as their mom directed, and soon all sat around the dining room table, the eat-in kitchen too tiny to be comfortable for more than two at most. The old oak dining room table had seen many a meal, many a homework assignment, many a conflict resolution, and many a celebration.

Jack's back rested against the ladder-back chair assigned since childhood, his seat ever since his mom had married the man who'd found and fallen in love with her after Jack's father's desertion.

Cecily's fiancé, Brian, occupied Jack's older stepbrother Matt's seat; half sister Brenna's remained empty. In the middle of finals, she'd be home when the semester was over.

"How's Brenna doing?" Jack asked, figuring that might be a safe conversation.

"Fine," his mother said. "She loves journalism. Competitive, but Brenna's got a special knack. So, tell us more about this girl you're bringing to the wedding. Is it serious?"

Jack stabbed a slab of medium-rare roast beef, lifting the slice from the platter to his plate. The center held just the right amount of pink. "Like I said, she's a vet. We just met."

"Meaning it'll fizzle," Cecily predicted.

"You don't know that," Jack snapped, suddenly irritated. "It's still new. You've known Brian forever, so what would you know about my relationships?"

Brian wisely concentrated on spooning green bean casserole onto his plate.

"So what color are her eyes?" Cecily challenged.

"Brown. With these little gold specks." The answer came forth automatically, without his having to think about it.

"Hmm. Okay, that was fast. You didn't turn on that recorder in your brain. Maybe you do actually like this one."

"I do." That wasn't a lie either, Jack realized as he reached for the mashed potato bowl coming his way. Kat was special. He easily recalled the length of her fingers and how they'd stroked Jingle's head.

He brought it all back—seeing the wide smile that indicated she'd had braces as a kid, for no one had teeth that straight. Full lips framed that perfect mouth, and he'd liked how the rose-colored corners crept upward when she saw something she liked. Little creases surrounded eyes that twinkled when she laughed. He made a big mound of potatoes on his plate and set the bowl in the middle of the table next to a small decorative Christmas tree. His mom had the decorations out early, probably on account of the upcoming wedding.

"Where'd she go to vet school?"

His brain found the answer quickly, seeing the diploma on the wall of her office. "Mizzou."

"My alma mater," Nelson noted. "Can't wait to meet her."

The gravy boat came Jack's way, and he used the ladle

to make a large brown pond in the center of his potatoes. "She's excited to meet all of you as well."

"I'm just excited you're finally bringing someone around," his mother said. "You never do."

"There's no point if he's not going to be serious about any of them," Cecily defended. "Which we know is most of the time. She must be special."

"She is," Jack confirmed.

"So where are you taking her next?" Cecily asked.

"What?"

"Like on a date. Surely she's not just hanging around waiting for my wedding. The food will be good, but not that great."

"We're attending the Pet Rescue Gala."

Cecily just arched an eyebrow. "The charity?"

"Our first public venture as a couple," Jack confirmed. "It's a great event. Black tie."

"Well, that will shock St. Louis's sensibilities to know that its calendar boy is off the market. I'll make sure to toss the bouquet her direction."

"Don't you dare." The words were out before Jack could stop them.

Cecily smirked. "Ah, now there's the Jack we know and love. So it's not that serious."

"We just met," Jack grit out again.

"Give your brother space," Jack's mom said. "He'll figure it out."

"Maybe," Cecily conceded. She gave him a long, assessing look. "Time will tell, won't it?"

Jack simply shoved another bite into his mouth to keep from replying.

#

By Friday evening, Kat turned into a complete basket case. This was not a real date. So why was she stressing over a silly charity ball?

Besides, it wasn't as if she hadn't seen Jack. He'd come by Monday morning at eight to get photos. He stopped by or called at least once a day to check on Jingle's progress. While the dog grew stronger day by day, Jingle still had a long way to go. He wasn't out of the woods, and he required constant monitoring.

Kat looked at her bed, now covered with dresses and one comfortable, sleeping calico kitten. "I tell you, Pippa, you're lucky you have a fur coat."

Pippa's black-tipped tail thumped once, her only acknowledgement of Kat's dilemma. She'd been so sure this morning. Wear her favorite dress, the red one with the slit up her leg. Until she remembered that Jack never forgot anything—and she'd worn it the night they'd met. So she tossed it on the bed and pulled out a deep green gown, only to find a stain on the skirt the dry cleaners had missed.

Two down. Then the black velvet standby looked too shabby, and everyone would be in black, a color that turned Kat's skin a ghostly shade of pale.

She even tried on the silver bridesmaid's dress she'd worn to her friend Marianne's wedding—until a glance in the mirror reminded her it shimmered like a cheap shower curtain, something a lot of wine at the reception had helped her forget. Time to donate that garment next time she cleaned out her closet. Dress five was another one she planned to donate—she'd worn it five years ago and it no longer fit. Dress six made her butt look big, and she couldn't remember why she'd bought it in the first place, unless she'd been indulging in retail therapy after her latest breakup. Her one shopping weakness post-breakup was buying pretty dresses.

Trouble was, she had very few places to wear them, but she'd purchase them anyway, just because she liked how wearing them made her feel. For a moment, she could pretend she was a radiant princess, or a supermodel, or an intelligent beauty queen, the type no man could resist.

Kat sat on the edge of her bed with a thump, the cat cracking one eyelid before closing it again. "You're no help," Kat told Pippa.

Frustrated, Kat dug freshly-painted fingernails into her thigh, all but her thumb crawling like a spider. She should wear the red dress. So what if he'd seen it? This wasn't a real date. Tonight she would have attended anyway because she believed so strongly in the work Pet Rescue did.

So red dress it was. Except for now the cat slept on it, and she'd need to take a lint brush to it.

Kat wrinkled her nose and frowned. Why was it that when nothing should matter, it always did? At least her hair had gone up into the knot without issues. Her hair, that unruly brown mess, hadn't disobeyed tonight. One small blessing.

Kat stood up, walked into the spare bedroom, and threw open the closet door. Surely she had something. Something she'd bought, intending to wear and shoved aside for some reason. She thumbed through, pushing hangers aside.

And there it was. She'd found the gown at the Women's Closet Exchange, a high-end resale shop. The dark blue silk fabric shimmered as she pulled it out. Why hadn't she thought of this dress first? She turned the hanger around. Oh yeah. Because the dress had no back. None whatsoever. The last time she'd thought about wearing it, she'd chickened out.

The fabric caught the light like moonlit water, and she decided to try it on. Kat tossed the hanger on the dresser and stepped into the dress. She pulled it up and over, the silk caressing her skin. She slid her arms through the slots, attached the back clasp that closed the two-inch collar. The full, floor-length skirt swished around her legs as she strode back into her bedroom and stood in front of the full-length mirror.

The back of the sleeveless dress hit the small curve of her back. The dress showcased a diamond-shape exposure of pale skin from under the strap collar to right above the V of her breasts. She adjusted the built-in bra cups and looked at her reflection.

The designer piece had been worn once according to the salesperson, and Kat had picked up the thousand-dollar gown for a mere fraction of that. She slid into the four-inch silver heels she brought out only for special occasions. Did she dare wear this? She felt utterly glamorous, but then again, she was revealing suggestive amounts of skin. She twirled, loving how the soft fabric swished.

Then froze as she heard the doorbell. Surely Jack couldn't be here already.

She cursed as she read the clock. Where had the time gone? She'd sworn she'd had at least another hour, not fifteen minutes. Blue fabric swishing, she walked down the front steps and let him in. "Hi."

"Hi," Jack said, his gaze sweeping over her. "Ready?"

"Almost," Kat replied, making her way back up the stairs. Jack gave a low whistle. "What?"

"That is one hell of a dress."

"Thank you," she said, a flush covering her cheeks. "I . . ."

"If you're trying to make a statement, you succeeded. I'll be the envy of every guy there."

She reached the living room and faced him. "It's too much. I can put the red one on and—"

"Don't you dare," Jack replied. His blue eyes had darkened to cobalt. "You're beautiful."

"Thank you," she replied again, and fled to her bedroom where she attached a sterling silver cuff bracelet, the only jewelry she'd wear aside from the matching dangle earrings.

She gave one last look-see in the mirror, put on a shimmery silver stole, and returned to the living room. Jack held out her black wool dress coat. "Shall we?"

"Definitely," Kat replied, stomach butterflies already abuzz. Beneath his coat he wore a black tux, and Kat caught herself before her mouth gaped open. She couldn't remember the last time she was this affected by a man, and that could spell trouble, for Kat had the sudden urge to yank him into her bedroom and let him slake the desire flowing through her, charity be darned. He held open the door to the stairs, and some cooler air blew in, clearing her brain.

"Lead the way," he told her, grin wicked. "It's going to be an interesting night."

And even "interesting" was too tame a word, Jack thought as he and Kat checked their overcoats outside the Ritz Carlton ballroom. Her dress was driving him to distraction. When he placed his hand on the small of her back, all five fingers found silken bare flesh. The gown was red carpet worthy, and worse, the way she wore it made parts of his body go into hyperdrive. When he'd followed her up her flat's front stairs, he'd mentally recited "Mary Had a Little Lamb"—anything to keep his lower half quiet. He was taking a lot of cold showers lately, both mentally and physically. She drove him mad.

Kat wobbled once in her heels as they entered the ballroom, and he cupped her bare arm to steady her, drawing her to him. She fit perfectly, which should worry his sensibilities. Yet, he hadn't one qualm or innate urge to flee. "We're over there," he said, bringing her over to a round table that sat ten. "Number thirteen."

"My lucky number," Kat murmured, as he pulled out the chair in front of the name placard reading Dr.

Katherine Saunders.

His fingers skimmed over the fine silver lace stole that covered her shoulder blades as he eased her chair in. His breath heated her ear as he leaned down and whispered, "It's warm in here."

She gave an involuntary shiver, as if the chair was slightly cool against her back. "It's fine," she told him. Her fingers trembled as she reached for the iced tea and took a long sip. Her eyes had also darkened, proving she was as sexually affected as he was. He was playing with fire.

"What do you want from the bar?" Jack asked, ready to retreat to safety.

"Red wine is fine," she answered.

"Be right back," Jack replied. Kat watched him leave, her gaze trailing over him.

"Handsome, isn't he? They don't make them much better than that." A woman dropped gracefully into the chair on Kat's right and held out her hand. "I'm Sharon. You here as Jack's date?"

"I am," Kat replied, keeping her tone even and the immediate, catlike hiss tamped down.

"Lucky you. Jack's quite a catch. Women have been after him for years but he's Mr. Elusive."

Kat took another sip of the iced tea, taking the moment to study the beautiful redhead whose black dress appeared painted on. She seemed pretty familiar with Jack. "How do you know him?"

Sharon laughed, long burgundy fingernails reaching for her water goblet. "Oh, I've known Jack for years. I'm married to Matt."

Tension whooshed from Kat, only to be replaced with confusion. "Matt?"

Sharon clearly found the whole situation amusing, as her perfect white smile spread ear to ear. "That would be so like Jack to not tell you a thing. Matt's Jack's older brother. Stepbrother, but it's been like twenty years, so past time to drop that moniker. Have you been dating long?"

"About a month," Kat replied, sticking to the story she and Jack had created.

Sharon suddenly snapped her fingers. "Oh, it's you." She pulled out her phone, turned it on. "I don't believe it. What luck! You're the wedding date."

"Uh . . ." Kat began as Sharon unlocked her phone and hit an app.

"At our final fitting, Cecily was telling us that Jack had a date. I can't believe I scored this coup. Here. Do you mind?"

She leaned into Kat's space, held up the phone, and took a quick picture. "Cecily doesn't believe you're real. This'll show her."

Kat sat dumbfounded as Sharon typed a message and hit send. Then she turned to the man approaching. He stood about five eight and had dark brown hair, the complete opposite of Jack. "Matt. This is Kat. Kat, this is my husband Matt. She's Jack's date. You know. The wedding date."

"Stop bothering my date," Jack inserted, arriving on the scene much to Kat's immediate relief. Jack handed her a glass of red wine and set down his longneck bottle of Bud. "Matt," he said, reaching forward to shake his stepbrother's outstretched hand. "Good to see you. Didn't know you'd be here."

"My firm is doing some of the pro bono work to assist the prosecuting attorney's office with task force issues."

"But you aren't involved in any of that," Jack pointed out.

"Yes, but I love auctions so I insisted we come," Sharon inserted, clearly smoothing the waters. "What a welcome surprise we're at the same table." She leaned over and squeezed Kat's hand. "We have been waiting to see Jack settle down for a long time." Kat resisted the urge to rub her hand; Sharon's grip had been a vise. "You do know, Jack, that your mom had a string of dates lined up for the wedding."

"So I heard. Someone ought to tell her that her matchmaking services are not required where I'm concerned."

"You know she's just trying to help. She's fixed lots of people up," Sharon told Kat.

"Then I'm lucky Kat rescued me." Jack dropped into the seat to Kat's left. He lifted her left hand to his lips and kissed the back of it, those blue eyes twinkling. A tremor of awareness shot through her, and she tamped it down. "She's my savior."

"That's me," Kat quipped as three other couples began to take their seats. "Always saving someone or something. This time it was Jack."

"That's sweet," Sharon said, and Kat could almost see her cataloging everything for later use. Matt, however, was clearly more cynical. His lawyer-trained gaze assessed her, and she resisted the urge to squirm.

"Oh that's right. You're the one with the illegal dog shelter," Matt said, putting two and two together. He took a sip of the dark cocktail as if his words weren't a bombshell.

"It's not illegal," Kat replied automatically, praying her tone sounded matter-of-fact and not defensive. She snaked her right hand forward, grabbing the wineglass as a shield.

"Kat is the vet who saved Jingle," Jack said, redirecting the conversation. His leg pressed against hers, and his right hand covered her left. To provide comfort, he squeezed gently. "Jingle's the worst abuse case I've ever seen, and Kat was the perfect person for the job."

"No one is questioning her ability as a vet," Matt replied.

"I personally inspected her shelter myself," Jack said, and Kat heard the underlying warning in his tone. "Did you not see the news report?"

"Boys," Sharon chided. "You should see them at family dinners," she told Kat with an apologetic smile. But at that moment Kat knew why she was really here, why Jack had come up with a silly fake dating scheme. Not only had he clearly failed to marry—which was the dumbest thing for anyone to ever criticize—but there was some undercurrent, some blatant tension between the two men. Kat didn't understand blended families, having never had one. But she recognized sibling rivalry as these two had it in spades.

"So, did I overhear that right?" a woman across the table asked. "You're the vet who saved that poor dog?"

Kat nodded. "I am."

"I couldn't believe that when I heard about what happened. We're making a huge donation in his honor. I couldn't bear if something happened to my Pookie. I'm Ellen Harper, by the way. This is my husband George."

Kat knew the name George Harper. More than likely her case was going to land in his courtroom. "Nice to meet you, Judge Harper."

"Indeed," he said, reaching for the salad plate in front of him, more interested in his food than her clinic.

Waiters came by with warm rolls, and soon entrée plates, and conversation shifted to topics like golf, vacations to Spain, Rams football, and Blues hockey. For the most part, Kat and Jack were able to contribute something to the table's cheery atmosphere.

Besides, the food was excellent and the wine smooth, and Kat went past her one glass limit by indulging in two. Perhaps that's why, despite the bareness of her skin, she felt so warm. Or maybe it was because Jack kept stroking the top of her arm—the searing heat making her flush. At one point during the speeches he draped his arm over her shoulders, his fingers twirling in the loose strands of hair at the base of her neck.

He was doing everything a boyfriend would do, and knowing Sharon watched their every move like a hawk, Kat allowed herself to relax and go with the flow. She had a part to play. Later she could remember this night wasn't real, no matter how authentic the desire her body exhibited. She blinked. She'd tuned out during the speeches, her body short-circuited by Jack's mesmerizing touch.

"So," the mayor was saying, "we are grateful to Jack Donovan for his deep commitment to making this partnership work. When Jeff proposed this joint task force a year ago, I didn't know how we would make the logistics feasible. But thanks to Jack, we have a road map and we've made a difference. So Jack," the mayor pointed to him, "thank you."

Kat clapped automatically as Jack stood, gave a brief wave to the crowd, and then sat back down. She leaned over to him. "That's wonderful."

Around the table, the others saluted him with raised glasses.

The mayor continued on a new vein, and Kat reached under the table to squeeze Jack's hand. She leaned to whisper in his ear, "Smile. Look happy."

He turned toward her. "I hate the attention—"

"I know," Kat replied, catching his mouth in a quick kiss because one, his mouth was right there mere inches away, and two, it seemed the right thing to do at the time to keep him from talking about how he hated all the attention.

Plus, he had good lips. Full. Tasty. Much better than the chocolate. Just a brief kiss before she pulled away, but his blue eyes had darkened and he'd brushed his blond hair off his forehead. Their hands had fused together, and he didn't make any attempt to let go. Kat leaned back, satisfied.

Jeff Andrews, Pet Rescue's Founder and CEO, and the man to whom the mayor had referred, spoke next, and he accompanied his speech with a slide show. The professional hockey player's wife who went out with Jeff once a month to look for stray dogs was in several slides. Jack was in one slide—carrying a puppy—and the rest of the show featured tons of photos of happy animals and adoptions.

The video hadn't relied on any gore, but it had tugged on everyone's heartstrings, and Kat knew St. Louis's elite would be opening their checkbooks wide tonight. As it was, regular tickets had started at $150 a plate. VIP tables had cost double that.

"Jack, your parents would be so proud," Sharon said as the various speeches ended. Next would be the silent auction and then dancing. "How exciting. Next year we must bring them."

"I'm just doing my job," Jack said.

"He's so humble," Sharon told Kat with a conspiratorial wink. "I need the ladies room. Come with?"

Kat wasn't a woman who needed to go anywhere in pairs, but she rose to her feet. Tonight was about family harmony, so accompanying Jack's sister-in-law fit the bill. She felt Jack's gaze on her backside until she turned out of sight.

No longer able to see Kat, Jack reached for his nearly empty beer bottle, lifted it to his lips, and drank the last, tiny unsatisfactory swig. Matt stared from across the table. "What?" Jack asked, setting the bottle down with a jarring thump.

Matt shook his head, disbelief clear. "What are you doing?"

"Finishing my beer," Jack replied with a shrug. "What's it look like?"

"I meant with Kat," Matt clarified.

Jack frowned and crossed his arms. "We're on a date. I would think that's obvious. You have to admit, she's a beautiful woman."

Matt fingered the short cocktail glass, rattled the ice. Jack kept waiting for a "She's out of your league" comment but received instead, "She's under legal scrutiny. It's a conflict of interest. You should be giving her a wide berth, pretty or not."

"I don't see any conflict and I like her," Jack replied, realizing he wasn't lying. He admired Kat. Found her funny. Charming. He enjoyed being around her. "I think she's special. And I haven't felt this way in well . . . years."

Matt exhaled. "Still. Couldn't you have waited until after her case gets settled?"

"When you met Sharon, would you have waited?" Jack paused for effect, not surprised when Matt stayed silent. "I like Kat a lot and that hasn't happened in a while. So why be subjected to matchmaking at Cecily's wedding when I can bring my own date, someone I care about?"

"I'm sure it doesn't hurt that you'll get Mom off your back."

Jack bristled. "That's not why I'm with Kat, and I'll find my own wife when I'm ready. Besides, you heard the mayor. He made me stand up and wave."

"He probably doesn't know you're dating her," Matt countered.

Jack's ire grew. He and Matt had been oil and water since their parents had first started dating. "And if he does, so what? He's been elected mayor for a record fourth term. I don't think my love life ranks high on his list of political concerns. You're the one who's always been worried about appearances. The only one who is most of the time."

"Pardon me for thinking of your career," Matt shot back.

Jack knew Matt meant well, but he'd heard this spiel or one like it enough times over the past twenty years. "Matt, that's why we're all South Side and you're in Ladue with kids in private schools. I'm a cop. I'll always be a cop. I like being a cop. I don't want to be anything else. I'm sorry if that doesn't meet your expectations of what I should be, or provide me an income that allows me to shop where you do or take vacations abroad. And I'm sure you've received nothing but grief over the calendar."

Jack drummed his fingers on the table. "Believe me, had I known the attention it gave me, I'd have found some way out. But what's done is done and it was for a good cause. I'm the one living with the fallout. Besides, everyone has some relative who's embarrassing. I'm yours."

Matt was one of the most skilled litigators in the city, but with his brother, he never had the right words. "I'm not saying being a cop isn't a noble profession. There are plenty of—"

Jack knew where this was leading and put a quick stop to it by cutting in. "Yes, but I've no desire to be a desk jockey. I don't want management. I'm a detective. I like working the streets and solving crimes. I like making a big difference, especially in the lives of animals. And I do. You heard the mayor."

Matt changed tactics. "You're blurring the lines of professionalism with—"

"With what? Romance?" Jack scoffed. "Give me some credit. I know what I'm doing. And if you're so worried, then put your money where your mouth is and help out."

"Help out?"

"You're the brilliant lawyer," Jack said, irritation growing. "Donate money. Time. Giving me some support might be a nice change of pace."

"I do support—" But at that moment, the women began to make their way back to the table and the men fell quiet, schooling their faces into neutral. Jack swallowed as Kat came closer, the beautiful dress turning heads as she wove her way through the crowd. He had the sudden urge to bundle her up, take her home, and ravage her until neither of them could move.

His hand tightened on the empty bottle. These were not thoughts he should be having, but like at the calendar ball where they'd first met, she called forth something primitive and primal from deep inside. Yet, he couldn't act on it. He was Mr. Bah Humbug.

None of this was real, and he was the wrong guy anyway, which meant there was a line they couldn't cross—one he wouldn't cross. He respected Kat too much. For Matt was right about one thing. Jack's track record sucked. Eventually all his relationships fizzled. So better to keep this as it was. Friends. No benefits other than getting his family off his back, which clearly, from Matt's attempt to be helpful, Jack was justified in doing.

He rose to his feet, overwhelmed with desire to touch her and knowing the one way he could legally do so. He reached for her hand as she came into range, tugged her to him, and bent his lips to her ear. "Come on, sweetheart. Let's dance."

Chapter Seven

Kat followed Jack onto the dance floor. He'd shed the tuxedo coat, unbuttoned the top shirt buttons, and loosened the black bow tie so that the ends draped on each side of the open collar. He pulled her to him, and their fronts fused as the band began a slow number.

His hands curved around her waist, resting on the bare skin above her hips. She experienced a delicious branding, the kind that seared with sensual heat. She snaked her arms up over his broad shoulders. *Oh Lord.*

Touching him made her weak.

The calendar had revealed all his upper torso assets, leaving little to the imagination. However, her imagination hadn't anticipated the reality of how those wide, muscular arms would really feel. Her traitorous body went into overdrive when her breasts pressed into that sculpted chest, causing anticipatory quivers that trembled through her like miniature earthquakes. His fingers toyed with the fabric seam, and her legs slid between his, moving in a step created since the dawn of time. Every nerve heightened; her heart skipped a beat.

She rested her head on his shoulder, drew in the scent of a woodsy aftershave. The starched shirt didn't scratch—she could have stayed in this delightful hazy trance all day. She'd danced many times, but never, ever, had her body longed for a man as it did Jack. Nestled in his arms, she felt safe. Cherished. He was strong, yet soft, and as she looked up, her gaze settled on the pure temptation that were his lips.

He drew her even closer, keeping her there as the band began another slow number. "So what did you and Sharon talk about?" he asked.

"This and that. She wanted to know how we'd met, how serious we were. I told her we'd fallen in love at first sight."

His exhale tickled her ear. "You are good."

He felt dreamy, and she fought from falling into that Cinderella-like, happily-ever-after fantasy that crept into every woman's head during a slow dance.

Kat drank in his scent again before forcing herself to ignore the warm, intoxicating glow—it wasn't real. She had to remember that. "Glad to be of help," she quipped. "After meeting Matt and Sharon, I can see why you needed me."

Fingers traced circles on the small of her back. "My family is a little intense."

"A little," she agreed, for while they had hidden it quickly, she'd seen the tension between the two men. "But sometimes families have very specific ideas."

"Mine has a mold, and I don't quite fit."

"Well, I like you just the way you are," Kat said, drawing back and brushing some microscopic lint off his shoulder as the song ended. "I wouldn't change a thing."

They stood there for a moment, gazes locked, until the music changed and the crowd began the electric slide, a St. Louis staple no matter how old the signature song was. Jack gestured. "Shall we look at the auction items?"

"Let's." Kat took his outstretched hand and followed him from the dance floor. She enjoyed the way her fingers fit into his as they began to look at the items, which ranged from some less than fifty-dollar pottery pieces to full-blown four-thousand-dollar vacations. She let go of Jack when she bent over a set of St. Louis Blues tickets and wrote down a bid. She set the pen down. "If nothing else, if I lose, someone else pays more. Every dollar counts. It's for the animals."

Jack looked around. "There's a lot of money in this room."

"Which is good for Pet Rescue and the animals," Kat replied, hearing his unspoken "too rich for my blood."

His arm made a sweep. "This doesn't intimidate you?"

"Why should it? I'm comfortable and I became a vet because I love animals, not because I wanted to be rich like my parents."

She bid on a handcrafted bead necklace running about seventy-five dollars. "This would be a perfect Christmas gift for my mother. I am a sucker for silent auctions. Do you know I have thirteen autographed baseballs?"

He gave her an odd look. "Do you even like baseball?"

She laughed. "Yes, and I go to the occasional game, although I admit I'm not a diehard fan. But I'm addicted to my collection."

"Well, then you might want that ball over there. Tony La Russa." Jack pointed out the former St. Louis Cardinal manager and Hall of Famer.

She sighed. "I have that one. He is a huge supporter and always donates. He has his own animal rescue foundation. Maybe that's the route I need to take."

"Let's not talk business tonight."

She stopped in front of an autographed book and wrote down a bid. "Okay. That's fair."

"I know the case upsets you. And you seemed to be enjoying yourself. I want us to have fun tonight."

"I am having a good time." They went to the bar and picked up new drinks. "It's been a nice evening. Best time I've had in years."

"I agree, and I hate these things. But you've made it tolerable. Highly enjoyable," he admitted.

"I'm glad."

"Me too." They wandered back to their table, a process that took a while as they kept stopping to socialize. Kat didn't mind. She liked watching Jack in action. He was a born leader, and clearly well respected. If she was being honest with herself, she also liked the way he moved and the way he filled out his tux. Judging from the appreciative glances he was getting, she wasn't the only one.

She bit the inside of her lip, a reminder not to forget.

She could lose herself in the moment far too easily. She had a bad habit—she often jumped in with both feet, never fully considering the consequences. It's how she'd ended up in her predicament with the shelter. Impulse often won over rationality, a trait she'd been trying to correct most of her life with little success.

This whole evening might not have been real, but she still wanted to kiss him. Her lips had quivered during the slow dance, her compulsion to touch overpowering. *Toss caution to the wind. Who cares if it won't lead anywhere!* She'd somehow managed to keep her wits.

"There you are." Sharon grabbed Kat's arm. "I have to check my items. Come with me."

Kat allowed herself to be propelled along to the first group of auction items, using the time away from Jack's magical presence to clear her thoughts and regroup. "What did you bid on?"

"This fabulous winery weekend in Napa. You?"

"A book. A necklace over there that my mom might like." *Nothing nearly that expensive*, Kat thought as Sharon upped her bid by a hundred dollars.

"We should check on them," Sharon said, but Jack approached, holding out Kat's sequined evening bag.

"You're buzzing," he said. "I didn't want to open it, but whoever's calling has tried multiple times."

Kat unlocked her phone, noting three missed calls and two texts. Her stomach dropped and her face drained of color. "We need to go."

"What's wrong?"

Her voice rose in a fevered pitch. "Jingle. The clinic. We have to go."

"What if you win?" Sharon asked, clearly confused.

"Buy it and I'll pay you back," Jack said, understanding the urgency. He grabbed Kat's hand and led her toward the exit. "I'll get the car while you retrieve our coats."

"Perfect." Kat took the claim ticket, and by the time she reached the front of the hotel the valet was holding the SUV door open. Jack put the siren on the roof, and within minutes they were at the back entrance to her clinic.

"Kat, thank God," the overnight vet tech said as Kat rushed into the OR. "I'm not sure what happened. Vitals were stable and then they plummeted . . ."

Jack didn't understand the medical jargon uttered next, and he stepped back as Kat pulled a surgical gown over her dress. She pointed to a small closet. "Jack, suit up. Scrubs are in there. I'm going to need you." She pulled a mask over her mouth.

"Sure thing." He peeled off the tuxedo coat, donned the green gown and a mask, and waited for instructions. While for the briefest moment at the ball Kat had been panicked, now she was in full control, as good and professional as any other first responder with whom he'd worked. "What do you need me to do?"

But Kat didn't answer; she was a flurry of activity as she worked on Jingle. She tapped a syringe to get the air out before slowly plunging the contents into the IV line. The dog, who had been trembling, immediately began to calm. Then she began to peel back the bandages. "Damn," she said, and as much as Jack wanted to ask, he kept his mouth shut, only asking for further information as needed after she issued him directions.

Kat and her tech worked well together, and Jack passed over this and that, until finally Kat wiped her brow and said, "That's it. All we can do. Now we wait again." Jingle lay sedated on the table as Kat turned to her tech. "Thanks Jane. You were great. Go home. I've got it from here."

The girl took off her gloves. "Are you sure?"

"Absolutely." Kat nodded. "Jack will help me."

"Thanks." The tech scrubbed out and left.

"So what happened?" Jack asked.

"Infection. I had to reclean one of the wounds. He's on an antibiotic but . . ." She stopped, clearly drained. "His body has a lot of recovery left to do. Can you help me move him? He's okay to pick up by lifting under his front legs and under his stomach."

Jack put Jingle back in his crate, and the dog seemed to sigh. "Good thing my cats won't miss me," Kat said, removing her scrubs and tossing them into the hamper. She glanced at her dress and sighed. "Some end to our evening. Thanks for staying and helping."

"Do you know how many times I've been called away on an emergency? I get it."

Most men she'd dated hadn't, Kat reflected, but Jack drew her close with a "Come here." His fingers found the knot on her left shoulder blade, and she practically moaned. "That feels so good."

"Least I can do," Jack replied. His phone pinged and he used his free hand to get it out of his pants pocket. "You won some of your items."

A tear slipped down Kat's cheek, and then she began to laugh as the weight of the evening crashed into her. "Yay," she quipped. "A bonus."

"Hey," Jack said. "It's okay. You saved him. And your dress is still beautiful. You're still beautiful." He turned her to face him and flicked away the stray tear with the rough pad of his finger. "How about I rustle up some food?"

"There's stuff in the break room. End of the hall," Kat told him. "Meet you there. Let me check his monitors."

She needed a moment to regroup. She made sure Jingle was fine, and then stopped in her private bathroom. Her updo had fallen. Her dress had wrinkled. Her right eye mimicked a raccoon's. Her lipstick had long faded. Taking a makeup wipe, she removed the black under-eye smudges, whisked away the last of her lip color. Then she took a quick swig of mouthwash and sighed.

She reached down and slid off the sanitary shoe covers and her heels, putting on the spare slippers she kept on the shelf. She had spare clothes in the closet, but no point. She'd rather change straight into the sweats she'd sleep in later. She padded toward the break room, where she discovered Jack microwaving frozen individual deep-dish pizzas. "Found these in the freezer." He held out a paper plate. "Hope you like plain cheese. It was this or some cheese rice thing with a green giant on the box."

Her mood lightened and she laughed. "Actually, I'll have you know that that cheese rice is pretty good. But this will be perfect."

A tickle of awareness passed between their fingertips as she took the plate. The microwave beeped, and Jack retrieved the second pizza. Kat sat at the small table, and Jack dropped into the chair beside her. He handed her a napkin. "There's silverware in that drawer," she said.

"Ah, no need. Fingers work." Jack lifted the four-inch circle and his lips closed around a bite. He pulled back and a string of melted cheese extended from mouth to finger. He wrapped it around the digit, stuck it in his mouth, then pulled his finger out with a pop. He grinned. "Good stuff."

Kat's legs clenched involuntarily as she watched his mouth work on his finger. No, *he* was the good stuff. He'd helped save Jingle again, simply rolling up his shirtsleeves and getting to work. Now he sat nonchalantly eating microwave pizza, the little dip to his chin catching another string of cheese, the edge of his lips wearing a dab of tomato sauce. She checked her hand's instinctive forward motion by lifting her own pizza. Instead, she pointed at her lips and chin, and he laughed and used the napkin to clean up. "Messy stuff, finger food."

"I offered you silverware."

"Real men don't use forks for pizza." He reached up and tugged off the bow tie, tossing the glossy black fabric on the table. "Annoying thing."

"Real men don't wear bow ties either?"

"Not while eating pizza."

117

She took a second bite, chewing slowly as the adrenaline of rescuing Jingle faded. Jack rose, went back to kitchenette, and returned with two glasses of ice water. "Thanks for helping."

He passed her a glass. "You look tired. Not quite the way we planned on ending the evening."

"Definitely not," she agreed, taking another bite. The warm gooeyness assaulted her taste buds, and for a second she closed her eyes in appreciation. "Almost better than the banquet food."

"Shock and awe does that to you. Until the adrenaline clears, you have heightened awareness. Extra energy. And an ability to think this pizza is gourmet."

"I guess you get adrenaline rushes all the time in your line of work."

"It happens." He nodded, thought back. "Yeah. Pretty much. To compensate, I'm a stress eater."

"You don't look it."

"I work out constantly to get rid of the excess energy. Supposedly it also helps relieve stress. And gives me biceps." He flexed and winked, looking silly and sexy at the same time. *Nice.*

"I wish it'd work that way for me."

His gaze roved over her, dropping to where the open diamond shape formed the V at the top of her breasts. "I'd say you have little to worry about."

"You're clearly delusional from tonight's adventure."

"Nope. Sharp as a tack. You handled yourself well. You knew just what to do. You were impressive."

"Practice and training," she replied. "Seriously. When I first started out, I had book knowledge, my schooling, and my on-the-job training, but it never truly prepares you, you know?"

"What's the worst mistake you made?"

"Thankfully, I haven't yet made a bad one and I pray I never do. Embarrassing, yes. This lady brought in her feral cat. Bad winter, so she'd brought him in after years of him living outside in one of those little igloos, complete with heating pad. I cleaned him up and looked him over, but it wasn't a comprehensive exam. So a few weeks later, the cat is still indoors, so she brings him in to be neutered. Thing is, he already was. I mean, I have this cat all sedated and there's nothing there. How did I not notice that the first time? How did I miss that?"

Jack laughed. "So what did you do?"

"I called her back, told her what was going on. He wasn't eartipped, so maybe he was someone's pet before he found her. She said he was about three when he came to live at her house. He'd been outside about eight years."

Jack shook his head. "That's crazy."

"Explains why he wasn't off carousing or defending his territory. He just lived on her porch. So we cleaned his teeth, and now he's the happiest indoor lap cat ever. But I check all cats thoroughly now."

"I've seen people think they have a girl kitten and it's a boy. Surprise."

"That happens too, but really, you can tell if you know what to look for. At least that's a mistake *I've* never made.

Knock wood."

Their pizza finished, Kat rose and threw away the empty paper plates. "Can I get you something else? Might be some cookies around here, and I know there's chocolate."

"I'm good," Jack said. "Unless you want something."

"It'd make me feel less guilty if you split a chocolate bar." She stood, rummaged in a refrigerator drawer, came out with a Hershey bar. Solid from cold, it cracked easily and she handed him half.

"Thanks." He broke the section into smaller portions and popped one into his mouth. "Even better than the cheesecake we ate tonight."

"I wouldn't go that far," she said. "Close second perhaps. That cheesecake was to die for."

"I second that, and few things are worth dying for. At least not food." He popped the last sliver into his mouth. "But it did hit the spot."

"So speaking of, what's next on your side of the agenda? Your sister's wedding, right?"

"Yes," Jack said. "Rehearsal Thursday and event on Friday. Two weekends from now."

"And we have my adoption event next weekend."

"I haven't forgotten."

But she could tell he wasn't enthused and worked to convince him. "Many of the previous adopters come with their pets, sort of like a reunion. It's inspiring."

"I wish it was that way all the time." They rose to their feet. "You staying here tonight?"

She nodded. "I have some sweats."

He touched her bare shoulder, the wispy silver stole long discarded. "Seems such a waste of a good dress."

She glanced at the crumpled mess. No need for him to know how many others lay discarded on her bed.

He reached for her hands. "Perhaps we should have one last dance."

"Here?"

"Why not? Didn't you say you were the romantic Hallmark movie type? Isn't that what the movie couple would be doing?"

She stammered, his touch short-circuiting. "Like you said, that is Hollywood magic."

"Tonight let's make our own magic. I've never seen anyone as dedicated as you. I'm proud you're on my team."

"Thanks," she said, her breath catching as he drew her into his arms. Warm, firm hands found her bare backside, and her heart raced. Without heels, her head rested on his chest and they swayed, like earlier, so in sync that she could almost hear the music. Her nails clung to the white tuxedo fabric, both stiff and soft at the same time. His jaw lined with sexy late-night stubble, and as she shifted, his lips found hers as if they'd been waiting the whole time for just such an opportunity.

Her mouth parted to welcome his feather-light ministrations, the light pressure more erotically tantalizing than a deep, sensual kiss. His delicate kisses skirted the edges of what each wanted, providing delicious hints of what could be, what might happen next should each choose to take the next step, choose to make fake dating truly real.

Her fingers wove into his hair, memorizing the silky texture. She longed to know more, so she slid her tongue along his roughened top lip before he parted and allowed her inside. He tasted of pizza, chocolate, and the promise of more.

Soft, came the thought, as most kisses she'd experienced had been hard and fast—as if they were on a race to the finish line. A prelude to sex. A foreplay necessity.

Kissing Jack was an impressive stand-alone act all by itself. The main event. Its own highlight. He deepened the kiss—touching his tongue to hers—the kiss never losing its sweetness. His slow, sensual plunder sent shivers throughout. She wanted him. All of him. Her breasts jutted forward. Heat pooled between her thighs. She didn't want to resist, but he was stepping away, running his fingers down her arms to keep some contact as he moved out of kissing range.

"I should probably go. You need sleep. You'll be up at the crack of dawn with Jingle."

"I will," she admitted, knowing he was right to stop, but her impulsive nature wanting to throw caution to the wind.

"I want you to know, the way you look in that dress is sinful. Pure temptation, and I'd like nothing more than to strip it off you." Her body trembled at those words, anticipating, wanting that up-close and personal interaction. "But I don't want this—us—to be casual sex. We said no emotions, but I like you. And I've never been able to separate sex from . . ." Fingers raked through his hair as he paused.

His heartfelt words touched her. "Me either. While we want each other, we don't want to mess things up. And if we like each other, we take each step slowly." Her impulsive nature wanted to rush, but she could see the wisdom in calming things down.

"Exactly." He drew her back into his arms, inhaled the scent of her hair, and then brought his lips back to hers, this kiss one that plundered before he groaned and pulled away. "I'm working tomorrow night. I'll call you."

"No need if it's a bother. I know how busy you are and—"

"I'll call you," he repeated. He released her, retrieved his tuxedo coat, and slid it on, cramming the bow tie into a pocket.

They made one more check on Jingle, who slept stable and sedated. Jack gave the dog a gentle pat on the head, and Kat walked Jack to the back door.

"Lock up," he said, pulling on his overcoat.

She nodded. "I always set the alarm."

"Good. You're in a safe neighborhood but—"

"Mom already gave me the lecture. Believe me, people think a vet clinic is a place to get drugs, so I'm wired with cameras recording. Better safe than sorry."

"A woman after my own heart. Sleep well." Jack gave her one last, brief kiss before he left. She threw the deadbolt and armed the system, watching on the monitor as he backed the SUV out of the parking lot. Then even his taillights disappeared from sight.

Her clinic was eerily quiet—most animals sleeping the night away. Tomorrow they'd be barking for food and attention, a symphony of chaos. The late-night silence normally soothed, but all of her senses were hyperaware. She pressed her fingers to puffy, well-ravaged lips, overcome by a sudden giddy quiver akin to the one she'd experienced at sixteen after her first real kiss.

She shook her head sharply, hoping to clear the delicious fog. When she'd signed on as Jack's temporary plus one, she'd ignored the fact that this might happen. That first kiss under the mistletoe should have been fair enough warning. Then, seeing him with Jingle . . . and after the way he kissed . . .

She rubbed her temples. She should have known better than to get involved, a tiny voice inside her head whispered, but honestly, she'd never ever heeded her inner warnings before. Besides, she'd promised to help rekindle Jack's Christmas spirit. Most importantly, she needed him for her adoption event.

And after all, what harm could a few kisses do?

So for now, she and Jack Donovan were going to spend a lot more time together. A deal was a deal.

She touched her lips again. As long as she kept her heart safe, with the way he kissed, she didn't mind one darn bit.

Chapter Eight

As St. Louis's only designated task force detective, Jack didn't keep regular hours. However, he did work a forty-hour week, often much more. He'd left Kat's clinic around midnight, and after watching a documentary on DVR because he'd been too wired to sleep, he'd finally crawled into bed around two a.m.

He'd turned off his alarm, letting himself sleep until noon, a ten-hour rarity. As the sheet slid low on his hips, he figured he'd be far more rested if he hadn't had erotic dreams of Kat.

That damn dress she'd worn the night before had been torture, and his imagination had peeled it off her and then filled in the blanks. He'd thus tossed and turned all night long.

He threw his legs over the bed, reached for his cellphone, and grimaced when he saw five missed calls—all from his mother. Sharon must have called her as soon as she woke up.

His phone buzzed and he turned on the ringer, and then slid his finger to the right, answering, "Mom." He paused, half listening as he padded into his kitchen. "Yes, I know. I slept in. No, Mom. Alone."

One-handed he uncapped the orange juice and sipped directly from the bottle. The phone slipped slightly and he jostled it back to his ear. "What? Repeat that."

"I said"—this time her voice came through loud and clear—"that Sharon seemed to like her. Anyway, I have her jewelry and book here."

He set the OJ aside, rummaged for one of those microwave breakfast sandwiches, and tossed it on the counter. "That was fast."

"Your father and Matt had a nine a.m. tee time. So tell me all about the ball."

He took another swig of juice, replaced the cap, and put it back. "Mom . . ."

"Better yet, bring her to dinner tomorrow night. I'm making pot roast."

"Mom." He sighed. No point in arguing with the human tornado. "I'll ask her."

"Great." His phone beeped, indicating another call. "Mom, gotta go. It's the precinct." He switched over, listened to the report. "Thanks."

He shoved the sandwich back in the freezer and headed for the bathroom. All the digital evidence had been confirmed, so warrants for the aunt and her boyfriend had been issued. Justice for Jingle could be served; Jack would make the arrests.

He called Kat from the car en route. She picked up on the third ring. "Hey, no time to talk, but head's up that you'll be getting media later."

"What for?"

"I'm going now to make the arrests in Jingle's case. I'd expect a media circus around four."

He heard her sigh. "Right when we close."

"I know. It's not ideal. My plan is to be there."

She sighed again, reminding him of the similar noises she'd made in his dreams. "Okay. Good luck. I'm glad they're getting what they deserve."

"Me too," Jack said. Contrary to what many people believed, arresting someone was a mixed bag. On one hand, he liked the sound of the handcuffs—that satisfying metal click as they locked onto the perpetrator's wrists.

However, the flip side was that he had to perform the act of putting on the cuffs in the first place—that the person he'd arrested had somehow lost a necessary piece of morality and done such a terrible thing to a defenseless, helpless animal.

Knowing he still felt sadness and compassion for the person—no matter how unrepentant or despicable that person was—was the only reason Jack knew he hadn't become jaded, that he hadn't let his anger and hatred overcome his sense of self. He felt sorry for the perpetrators—not that they didn't deserve to be arrested (for that they did), but he pitied them for being such a poor example of the human race.

So he tuned out the "It was just a damn dog! You can't

do this!" shrieks of the aunt as he loaded her into the back of the patrol car, banged on the roof, and let the officers take her to the station. The boyfriend, who already had a long rap sheet going back to juvie, went a lot quieter. Jack figured he'd owe the guys transporting the hysterical aunt a round of beer.

"So she done it, huh?"

Jack glanced down to see Peter standing behind him on the front sidewalk. "She did, yes."

"Got the proof?"

Jack nodded. "We wouldn't have arrested her if we didn't have solid evidence."

Peter used the toe of his shoe to scratch some gravel, gathered where the concrete had cracked. "She gonna go to jail?"

"That'll be up to the jury," Jack said.

"But you hope so, huh?" Jack bit back his retort as Peter kept talking. "Don't blame you. Lots around here think like she do, that it's just a dog. But my momma say you don't do that to no animal." He gave a shudder. "I'd hate something like that happen to Buttercup."

Jack wasn't quite sure what type of pet Buttercup was, but it didn't matter. "Your mom sounds like a very wise lady to me, Peter."

He beamed. "You remembered my name."

Jack pointed to his forehead. "I remember everything. So I only want to hear good things about you, got that?"

"Yes sir." Peter shoved bare hands into his coat pocket. The day was windy and cold, and the coat looked worse for the wear. "Dog gonna make it?"

Jack thought of last night, when Jingle had relapsed, and revisited in his mind the sight of Kat, standing there in her scrub-covered dress, working frantically to stabilize him. "I sure hope so," he said. "The vet is doing all she can."

"I hope so too," Peter said with a nod, walking with Jack to his SUV. "Me too."

Jack arrived at Kat's clinic a few minutes before four and found the major St. Louis media outlets already camped out in the front lot or parked on the side street. The police had managed to keep the arrests quiet, preferring not to have that event filmed. However, one enterprising new outlet had been outside the precinct doors, so they might have some footage of the arrestees being moved inside the station. The media would all air the arresting mug shots.

Jack drove around to the back and buzzed the door. Louise let him in. "Hey, I wanted to talk to Kat before we face that circus."

"She's finishing up with a patient."

"I'll wait. How's Jingle? Can I see him?"

Louise's lips thinned but she nodded. "This way." She took him by the kennel where he'd placed Jingle last night. "She's kept him sedated. She had to clean out that one burn wound again, and that hurts."

Jack noted that Jingle's breathing seemed steady. "Poor dog." He leaned over the puppy. "Hey buddy. How you

129

doing?" He stroked the dog's head. "I got them for you. Just like I promised. No one will ever hurt you again."

"So you arrested them?" Kat stepped into view, and he straightened, caught baby talking. Her hair was up in a ponytail, her face bare except for some mascara and a shimmery neutral lip gloss. Her white lab coat covered a blue oxford, collared shirt embroidered with the clinic logo over her heart. She wore a pair of black pants. Even without the fancy dress and hairstyle, she was gorgeous. He resisted the urge to pull her in her arms and kiss her senseless.

So instead, he kept things professional. "I did."

She nodded, satisfied. "Good. Let me just wash my hands and we can go face the horde. They've been there for an hour. My clients are flustered. The neighborhood association president called to tell me it was another disruption."

"But we actually have new clients because of Jingle and the media," Louise told Jack as they all walked through the small vet area and toward the lobby.

"Yes, but now the association has one more thing to add to its list of complaints. My lawyer already called about this, too. Can't win for trying," Kat said. She stopped at the sink to wash her hands. "Okay, let's do this so they go away."

"Wait," Jack said. On her lab coat, she'd attached three small Christmas pins: a tree, an angel, and a gingerbread man. The latter was upside down. "Hold up a minute."

He adjusted her pin, his fingers tugging the lab coat

and her toward him. Then he reached to her left temple and removed a piece of gray cat fur from her hair.

He held the tuft out, and she put it in the trashcan. "One of the hazards of the job. Last patient was a bit of a shedder."

"You look great," Jack said as they stepped into the empty lobby. "It's quite cold out there, so how about we let them in? You'd look good with the tree in the background."

"You're the expert with the media training."

"Then let me control this."

"Okay."

A moment of trust passed between them, and Jack opened the clinic doors so the reporters and their cameramen could come into the room. Jack assigned them places.

"Quite the organizer," Louise commented. "And how he removed that fuzz and turned your pin—"

"Out," Kat hissed, and Louise laughed. "Go check on something."

"Dr. Saunders? Ready?" Jack reached his arm out, motioning her to join him.

She stepped forward, ready as she'd ever be, and nodded.

"Ladies and Gentlemen of the press," Jack began as microphones went into this face, "thanks for joining me here at the Chippewa Animal Clinic, where late last night Dr. Katherine Saunders worked to once again save Jingle's life. Jingle wouldn't be in this precarious state if it hadn't been for two people who doused him in gasoline and set him on fire. Today I am pleased to announce that arrests have been made in conjunction with this heinous crime."

As Jack continued to talk, Kat found herself mesmerized. His voice contained authority and decisiveness. He spoke clearly, calmly—outlining the crime, the perpetrators' reasons behind their actions, and his own refutation of the perps' arguments. Kat could see the media lapping up every word. Justice for Jingle already had a large Facebook following; she had no doubt the number of page likes would quadruple after tonight's news broadcasts.

"Now Dr. Saunders will give you an update on Jingle's condition," Jack said, turning the press conference over to her.

"Jingle is recovering from infections, and I'm cautiously optimistic," Kat told the reporters. "He still has a long way to go, including skin grafts."

"When will he be able to be adopted?"

"We're in no position to determine that yet. Healing takes time."

"Dr. Saunders has provided Jingle with excellent free medical care," Jack added.

"Have you heard anything more about your lawsuit?" a reporter shot out.

Kat's stomach clenched, but she'd been expecting this question ever since Jack called her. So she told the truth. "My court date is the Monday before Christmas."

"Do you expect to win?"

She leveled her gaze. "As with Jingle, I'm cautiously

optimistic. Animals need tender loving care, and I provide that and a home until they find their forever family. To help provide a forever home, my annual adoption event is next Saturday. So come on by then."

"I'll be here signing calendars," Jack added, giving the cameras his trademark grin. "It's the least I can do for Jingle and all the pet charities the purchase of this calendar benefits."

And with that, he called an end to the questions, and the reporters left. "We'll see if that last part makes the news," he said as they watched the news crews drive away.

"It'd be great publicity."

He tucked a stray strand behind her ear. "Yes, it would. So the Monday before Christmas."

A sad breath left her. "Yeah. One of the last on the docket, my lawyer told me. They want it wrapped up before the holiday. So it could either be a very merry Christmas or very bah humbug. I'm praying for the first one. All I want for Christmas is that shelter license."

"Fingers crossed." He made the gesture with his right hand. "I've got to hit the road. Wish I could stay, but I'm on stakeout tonight."

"Sounds exciting."

"Not really. We're busting an illegal animal fighting ring."

She shuddered. "Dogs?"

He shook his head, sending that sandy blond hair over his forehead. "Cockfighting."

Disbelief that something so barbaric could be

133

happening in St. Louis had her saying, "You're kidding me."

A short scoff accompanied, "I wish I was. It's a lot more widespread than people think. A few days ago they busted a three-state fighting ring in the south. People drove for miles to watch the fights and bet. Worse, they brought their kids. Who brings kids somewhere they attach blades to the birds' beaks so they do more damage? It's sickening."

Kat shuddered again. "I'm glad you'll be there to stop it. What will happen to the birds?"

"The Humane Society of Missouri's animal cruelty task force will be there too. They'll take all the animals."

"That's good." She shifted her weight as conversation wound down. Did she kiss him good-bye?

He made the choice, giving her a quick peck on the forehead. "You did a great interview. I'll talk to you tomorrow. Text me if you need me or if anything happens to Jingle."

"I will."

Then he was out the front door, taking the outside route to the SUV parked behind the building.

"He didn't stay long," Louise observed as she returned.

"He has to work tonight."

"It's Saturday."

Kat crossed her arms. "Animal abuse doesn't take a holiday."

"So you two seem tight."

"I guess working to save a dog will do that."

Louise grinned. "Sure it can't be more?"

Kat shook her head. "We're friends. With all that's going on, that might be the best place for us."

Louise scoffed. "He's hot. How can you say that? Go for it."

Kat had considered all this. Processing her feelings for Jack had kept her up most of the night. "And then what? Awkward conversations at all the places I have to see him?"

"No gain without risk."

"I truly hate you at times."

"I know," Louise laughed. "But really, what do you have to lose?"

My heart? Kat headed back to check on Jingle. Jack Donovan was the type of man she'd fall for, and Mr. December was also Mr. Wrong. He'd made it clear that the only reason he'd wanted a relationship was to keep his family from trying to hook him up at the wedding. She was a fixer, so she'd come up with her own scheme not to be alone. Her parents were just as overbearing.

She and Jack would end. That was as certain as sunrise. Better to keep any deep feelings to a minimum, similar to what she had to do for the animals in her care. She loved her animals, but she had to let them go. Jack would be no different. The more involved she became, the harder it would be to separate.

Jingle was resting as comfortably as he could under the circumstances. Angela approached. "You need to get out of here. We've got closing and watching Jingle."

Home sounded nice. "I would like to see my cats."

"And they'd like to see you," Angela replied. She

touched Kat's arm reassuringly. "We will call if anything goes wrong. You know that. Go. We've got this."

Kat went home, poured herself a glass of merlot, reheated take-out, and plopped herself in front of the television. Around seven thirty, her cell phone beeped, indicating the clinic's emergency line had received a voice message and forwarded it.

She dialed in to listen, knowing it had to be a patient. Her staff would have called her directly. "Kat? I'm sorry, I didn't know how to get ahold of you and Jack's not answering. Is he with you? Are you coming to dinner tomorrow night? I'll kill him if he didn't invite you. I have your jewelry and your book. Oh, this is Jack's mom. Joyce."

Joyce rattled off her phone number, and Kat grabbed for a pen. She wrote the number down and cleared the message. On one hand, not a pet emergency she needed to deal with. That was a relief. On the other, that was Jack's mother. Jack hadn't invited her to dinner. Did he not want her to go? Was he working tomorrow night too? Was this something she should have known about?

She sighed, realizing this is why she hated relationships, even fake ones that were supposed to be simple.

She sent Jack a text message, but after thirty minutes he still hadn't answered. As the clock crept closer to nine, she reached for her phone and dialed Joyce's number.

"Kat!" Joyce said as she introduced herself. "I feel as if I know you already."

"Uh . . ." Maybe calling Jack's mom wasn't such a good

idea.

"Sharon brought me your auction loot and said you wore a lovely blue dress. So dinner tomorrow?"

"Jack didn't mention it. He's on a stakeout. That's why he hasn't called."

Joyce wasn't to be deterred. "So you'll come?"

"Jack—"

"Hasn't dated anyone in two years. Not since Julie, who dumped him after a five-year stint. I'm sure he's told you about that."

"Uh," Kat began, but Joyce charged on.

"She certainly wasn't the one for him and we were all very relieved when he didn't get engaged after her ultimatum. So dinner?"

Kat tried to regain control. "I need to talk to Jack. He may be working."

"Do you have plans?" his mother asked.

"Well, no but—"

"Then you come even if he can't."

"This relationship is rather new and . . ." Kat paused. She had no clue what to say. Would this hurt Jack or help him?

Joyce sensed her hesitation and went for the kill. "You're sitting with family at his sister's wedding. Wouldn't you like to meet us all first?"

"Um . . ."

Joyce added some enticement. "Dinner's on the table at five thirty sharp. Pot roast. I'm told I make the best roast in the city. I'll set you a plate."

And before Kat could decline, Joyce disconnected. Kat stared mindlessly at her phone, swiping through her apps as if they could magically provide the answer. Finally she sent Jack a text: "Your mom called me. Dinner five thirty tomorrow. Pick me up at five unless you have a good excuse to get us out of this. Although pot roast sounds good."

She set her phone aside and flipped the television to TLC, which was showing a *Say Yes to the Dress* marathon. Kat watched about ten minutes before turning the channel to TNT, which was showing an eighties action-adventure movie. *No use wishing for what wasn't going to happen anytime soon.*

Sure, she'd dated, but most of her relationships fizzled after a month or two—work always came first. First, she didn't date any guys who didn't like pets. Pets were non-negotiable. Second, few men wanted to come second to her practice, but she refused to sacrifice her life's work for a man. The dating pool was minuscule at best.

A commercial came on, so she flipped back to TLC to see a bride say yes to her dream dress. Kat hadn't known Jack had been in a long-term relationship. He'd simply said he needed his parents off his back. She understood that—every time she spoke to her mother, she always asked about her relationships or bemoaned Kat's lack thereof, and Kat knew that this Christmas the pressure would be on as her mother had gotten the idea that she'd like to be a grandma someday, especially when she got back from her trip.

Kat turned off the TV, deciding to go to bed early. While the accommodations in her office were nice, sleeping in her own bed would be wonderful and the extra sleep would do her good. She set the news to record and, after picking up Pippa, headed for bed.

***

Jack had never seen so many feathers. Okay, maybe when he and Matt had gotten into that one big fight and destroyed his mother's down pillows. Maybe then.

But he hadn't been covered with them, although he had gotten a good spanking. "Catch that!" someone called.

"Got it," Jack called, reaching down to grab a black rooster. Immediately the bird turned its beak and began pecking at the heavy gloves Jack wore. Jack gripped the squirming bird and dropped it into an open-top cage. Quickly someone else closed the lid on the now flapping bird.

"Never thought I'd be doing this in the academy," Mike quipped.

"Me either," Jack admitted as a Humane Society of Missouri rescue worker carried the crate away. Over twenty birds were all on their way to the Longmeadow Rescue Ranch out in Union, where they'd be evaluated and cared for. "But it's worth it."

Five ringleaders and more than twenty participants had been rounded up and arrested. Caught red-handed and videotaped. The prosecutor would take the case from here.

He surveyed the empty building, committing the

space to memory.

"That's all of them," Mike said.

"Good," Jack replied.

"I'm never going to own chickens," Mike said. "Got my workout chasing them. Enough for a lifetime. Heck, might not even eat them again."

Jack removed his gloves. "Agreed." He approached the Humane Society lead to coordinate a few, final things. Then he was free to leave the scene, the uniformed officers doing the final touches like putting up police tape and evidence gathering. Despite the December chill, Jack wiped his forehead, not surprised to find a feather stuck to face. He flicked it to the floor and headed to the SUV, Mike already there waiting for a ride back to the precinct.

"Am I clean?" Jack asked.

Mike walked around him, picking a few feathers off his back and pointing out others that Jack removed himself. "Thanks. I don't want to have to detail the car."

For warmth, Mike blew on his now bare hands, the heavy, animal-handling gloves removed. "I'm just grateful we don't have to transport any of those cluckers. Can you imagine how loud that van's gonna be?"

Jack shuddered. The noise in the barn had been excruciating. He couldn't imagine having squawking roosters in the back. Relishing the silence, he and Mike didn't even turn the radio on.

They reached the police station, where Jack and Mike filed their reports. By the time Jack caught a minute and pulled out his phone, it was almost six a.m. and he had several messages. He read Kat's text and frowned. After listening to his voice mail, his frown deepened. His underhanded mother had circumvented him quite nicely. Jack rubbed the nape of his neck.

"Hey, up for breakfast?" Mike asked. "Some of the guys are headed to Uncle Bill's."

"Yeah," Jack replied, thinking that Kat would be up soon, so he could call her before he got some shut-eye. Breakfast sounded like a plan. "Let's go."

***

Kat woke to the sound of her doorbell and grimaced. Her clock read a little past eight o'clock. First, who was calling this early? Second, she'd overslept.

Even on her day off, she'd normally be awake by six. She'd run a mile or two on the treadmill, shower, and go to the clinic to check on her patients. While today was her partner's turn for rounds, with a patient like Jingle, she'd go in herself too.

The ceramic tile of her foyer felt cold as she padded to her front door. She could see the figure through the stained glass. Not someone selling something. *Jack.*

She tugged the door open, letting in a blast of arctic air that made her nipples pebble. She crossed her arms over the thin tank top—the way his blue eyes had darkened revealed he'd gotten a good look. "What are you doing here?"

He stamped his feet on the porch. "Is someone here? I

didn't think . . ."

Her yoga pants rode low on her hips. "No, even in fake dating I'm monogamous. It's just me and my cats. You're letting all the heat out. Come in."

"Thanks. Figured we needed to talk about tonight."

"You couldn't just call?"

He shook his head, the blond hair falling in his face. "I'm exhausted. Haven't slept yet. I have a tendency to not make sense when I talk on the phone tired."

They stood in the tiny four-foot-square landing, and as she was barefooted, he towered over her. She reached up, realizing her hair was a bird's nest, and then realized her mistake. The ribbed tank molded to her breast, her nipple still protruding.

"Uh . . ." She eased past him, back up the stairs, highly aware of the scanty material she wore. Jack followed, Pippa attacking his heels the moment he stepped into the living room. "Can I get you some coffee?"

"No, I'm good. Had four cups with breakfast. Uncle Bill's." He raked a hand through his hair, the blond strands plastering. He had a full stubble beard. He wore blue jeans, down jacket emblazoned with the St. Louis Police Department logo, and he rubbed his hands together. "We do not have to do this tonight."

She blinked. "Your parents?"

"Yes." He shoved his hands into his pockets lest he touch her. "We do not have to go to dinner."

"Look, I knew what I signed up for. If this gets your family off your back, I'm game."

"Really?"

She nodded. "You haven't met my family yet, and I'm sure I'll owe you after the chaos of next weekend."

He closed his eyes for a second and groaned. "The pet adoption."

"Exactly. You're my celebrity guest." She gave him an encouraging smile. "So why don't you go get some sleep and pick me up at five?"

He couldn't resist. He reached for her, dragged her into his arms for a big hug. *Big mistake.* The thin material she wore concealed little, making him instantly hard. Her unfettered breasts crushed against his chest, and he clutched the silky fabric at the small of her back, gathering her to him as he brought his mouth to hers.

She tasted delicious; he drank in her sweetness as he deepened the kiss. He expected her to draw back, and when she didn't, one kiss stretched into another. Two became three. Three turned into four. He slid his hands lower, cupping her bottom and dragging her pelvis against his.

"You were sleepy," she said, her hands on the lapels of his police jacket.

He slid his mouth down her neck, loving the trembles his lips left in their wake. "Who needs sleep?"

Her hands found his chest, and she let out a shiver as his lips trailed along her collarbone. She rubbed against his hard length. "Oh." Her whole body shook, and her next "Oh" dragged out longer.

"Like that?"

"Mmm, hmm," her voice was suddenly an octave lower. She arched her neck, allowing his lips lower. He curved a finger under the spaghetti strap, sliding it down over the swell of her breast. He found her nipple and circled the nub. She cried out again and pressed closer to him, her need evident.

He slid his hand into her top, cupping her breast and bringing the straining nipple to his mouth. He drew it inside, and her breath hissed. With his free hand he cupped her bottom closer to him, locking her hips onto his so he could increase the friction by inserting his leg between hers. He then pulled the other part of her top down so he could suck one breast while he rolled the other between his fingers.

She arched back, and he took the silky fabric and rubbed it across her nipple. He resumed circling her areola with his tongue. She trembled and he sucked deeper, sending her over the edge. "I've never . . . like this . . ." She lost words as he shifted his leg, creating more friction. A primal surge shot through him—he'd made her this out of control, this turned on, this responsive.

Little cries came from the back of her throat as she shattered in his arms. He wanted to explore her wetness— taste her sweetness—but he settled for recapturing her lips and keeping her upright as her legs had turned to jelly. A part of him throbbed with need. All he had to do was move his hand lower and he could lay her back on the couch and . . .

But he had not come here for that. Passion could easily sweep you away—and every time he saw Kat, she tore down parts of his defenses, took down walls he'd built to surround his heart. He wanted no regrets. For either of them.

Brown eyes he could drown in opened and blinked as she came down from the high. He kissed her again—gentler, softer. "Oh."

"Good?"

"Uh-huh." She nodded. "Your fingers are magical. That was—"

"Fabulous." He finished, his mouth back on hers for another taste. "Don't you dare say it was a mistake."

A mistake? *Hell no.* Kat wanted more, and she reached for him, but he caught her fingers before she made contact below his belt. "If you touch me, I'll explode."

"And that's a bad thing?"

He reached his hands into her hair and brought his mouth down for another crushing kiss. "I haven't showered. I'm a mess. I've had no sleep. I want you. But not like this."

"Huh?"

"I didn't come here to make love to you. Not that I don't want to. I want nothing more. But our situation is complicated and I haven't even romanced you." He winced. "Did that come out right?"

"Jury is still out. You got me all hot and bothered and—"

"Shh." He put a finger to her lips. "You are beautiful. I want you. But you deserve . . ." He paused—for a man who could remember everything, finding the right words

Michele Dunaway

shouldn't be so difficult.

She frowned. "Deserve what?"

"More." He thrust his hands into his pockets. "I don't have a good track record. I'm not looking for commitment. But friends with benefits sounds somehow cheap. Much less than you deserve."

Kat crossed her arms. As much as she appreciated Jack's calling a halt, part of her wished he hadn't. "So what do you propose?"

"Let's slow this down. See how things unfold." The pink silk hugging her breasts made him inwardly groan. He wanted to sink inside her and find the release he craved, and damn the consequences. But his mother had raised a gentleman. Kat deserved better than a roll in the hay. She deserved better than him, too, but he ignored that. "If we change the rules, it shouldn't be because we gave into a moment of passion. Because I don't want any regrets between us."

"That's fair," Kat said. She could respect him for that.

He turned, took a step toward the door, clearly reluctant to go. "You said you liked pot roast?"

"Love it," Kat said.

"Then I'll pick you up at five."

Chapter Nine

"We've got a good crowd," Louise noted the following Saturday. Not yet nine a.m., and the clinic parking lot was full; the lobby was packed. Vet techs wearing elf hats passed out candy canes. A fat, white-bearded Santa Claus sat by the Christmas tree, and an elf assistant stood by ready to take both human and pet photographs with jolly St. Nick.

They'd brought the adoptable animals into the lobby and cleared a way to a special area devoted to cats. The patient rooms had been set aside for getting-to-know-you time. Everyone was working today, including a small army of volunteers who held leashes to very excited, yapping dogs, each one hoping for a new family. The fundraising committee had helpfully sent a huge stack of calendars, and already they'd sold thirteen. Kat expected them to fly off the shelf once Jack arrived.

"Where is Mr. December?" Louise asked, as if reading Kat's thoughts.

"He'll be here at ten." At least that's what he'd told her

last night over the phone. After being all hot and heavy Sunday morning, Jack had then kept his distance, giving her a chaste kiss good night after his family dinner, a dinner that had been interesting to say the least. She'd liked Jack's family—a rowdy and raucous bunch who threw things out there, unlike her family functions, which were much quieter and more sedate. And the pot roast had been delicious.

This week Jack had been busy with investigations, and while he called daily to check on Jingle, he hadn't been by the clinic. That made sense, Kat knew. No need to be joined at the hip, and already the deep timber of his voice had her anticipating his phone calls. She'd discovered how easily she could fall into bed with Jack—no way should she risk falling for a man who made it clear he didn't want any type of long-term commitment, something she eventually did want. Perhaps her New Year's resolution should be to get back out there. Time to stop making excuses, like telling herself she'd never find Mr. Right, so why bother trying?

"Kat, this is Mrs. Schneider and her daughter Lizzy. They're interested in an older cat." Angela stood there with a woman and child.

"Black kitty," Lizzy, who looked about three, insisted.

"She's rather rambunctious. I thought an older cat might be more able to tolerate her enthusiastic petting than a hyper kitten," Angela suggested.

"A good idea," Kat agreed, "especially as you can tell an older cat's temperament much better than a kitten's.

Have you ever had a cat before?"

"I had them growing up," Mrs. Schneider said. "It's just me and Lizzy at home, and now that's she's older, I told her we could get a cat for Christmas."

Lizzy danced on one foot as Kat held out her hand. "Come with me. I have the perfect cat for you." She led them back to the cat area and stopped in front of a big black and white tuxedo cat. "This is Jinx. He loves kids."

Lizzy held out her fingers, and the cat eased forward to sniff. "Jinx. Hi Jinx!"

She stuck her fingers through the wires, and the cat rubbed against them. Lizzy laughed.

"How about we put you in a room and take him out of his crate?" Kat asked. "He's neutered and up-to-date on all his shots."

"My kitty," Lizzy said, fingers still stretched through the wire.

"Let's," Mrs. Schneider agreed. "He's a pretty cat. We may just have found the one for us."

Kat called for a volunteer, who took everyone to get acquainted. Then she turned to see Jack there staring at her oddly.

"Hi. Glad you made it."

"Quite the crowd." Jack observed. His hands remained in his pockets, tension obvious.

"More than last year. I'm very hopeful. Our goal is to clear the shelter and place every animal." Kat drank him in. He wore a maroon flannel shirt tucked into fitted blue jeans, showing his very nice backside. His blond hair was swept back, making him every bit the hot Mr. December of the calendar, albeit with more clothes. "They are going to gobble you up," she said.

The corners of his lips twitched. "Sounds so appealing . . . Unless you're planning some gobbling yourself."

She flushed with giddy heat and checked the automatic "Maybe later." She had to be professional. Instead she said, "I know this is difficult for you." She gestured around. "But just wait and see. I'll think you'll be pleasantly surprised."

"Which is why I'm here." She waited. "And for you," he added with the hint of a smile. "How's Jingle doing? I've missed him."

"He's turned a corner. Jeff Andrews called to see when he'll be ready for adoption, but we're months away, so he's staying put. However, he convinced me to show him to the media next week. He said we need to keep his progress in the news."

"Definitely."

A volunteer poked her head in. "Kat, we have another adopter who'd like a cat."

"Coming. Can you show Jack where the calendar table is?"

"Sure."

"That's your cue."

Jack followed a woman he didn't recognize out to a small folding table that had been staged with two black Sharpie markers and huge stacks of calendars. Immediately a small queue formed, and as the volunteer assisted, Jack lost sight of Kat. He had a pretty steady flow of traffic, and two hours later his hand hurt. He'd easily signed more than two hundred calendars.

"Cookie?"

He recognized that voice. Knew it well. "Mom? What are you doing here?"

She held out a green platter with an assortment of edibles. "Surprise! We came to support Kat. Figured she might need some sustenance. Also Sharon and Matt are here for a dog. Surely you remember? Or weren't you paying attention Sunday when they were discussing that they might adopt a pet?"

Jack leaned around to see his nephew Matthew jumping up and down. The entire family had shown up for pot roast, making the table crowded. He thought back, reviewing the conversation like replaying a movie. "Oh yeah." His attention had been elsewhere. His leg had been pressed next to Kat's, and he'd been close enough to have a view down her shirt, which had caused him to relive how he'd rolled his tongue over her breasts and . . .

"Earth to Jack." His mom waved a hand in front of his face. "I'm also here because I need ten calendars and you still haven't brought them by the house."

That had been a deliberate oversight on his part. She set the cookies down and began to count on her fingers. "It's not everyday your son is a local hero. There's my three sisters, my friends Betty, Pam, Lisa . . . better give me eleven to be safe. I have a list somewhere. Might need more."

Lovely. Now everyone would be staring at him half naked next Christmas.

She rummaged through her Mary Poppins purse for the list, and Jack uncapped the Sharpie marker. Matt, Sharon and Matthew left to find a full-grown dog. He couldn't see his staid brother dealing with house training a puppy.

He signed all his mother's calendars, and then much to his relief, she went off to help pick out the dog. There were five calendars left, and those sold quickly. He was done. He stretched out his legs and leaned back in the plastic chair.

His watch read noon. Kat's event would run for another four hours, but she'd told him he didn't need to stay. He surveyed the scene. People with and without pets posed with Santa. A jar marked For Jingle contained loose change and bills—he could see at least one twenty and several fives. Under the tree, people placed unwrapped pet items to be donated to shelter pets. All around workers had clipboards with adoption applications. It was like being at an auction—you couldn't help but want to buy something and take it home.

Into this fray entered two men. Jack recognized one from his research. Fred Fennewald. Head of the neighborhood association. The other had his phone out, recording. Jack rose to his feet, went to greet both. "Fred," Jack held out his hand. "Detective Jack Donovan. Nice to meet you."

Fred's hand was a limp fish as the men shook. "You're

that detective. You're the one who dismissed my complaint."

"Yes," Jack said amiably, giving Fred's hand a firm squeeze before he let go. "Here to adopt a pet?"

"I have three Shih Tzus."

"Then a photo with Santa?" Jack offered, pointing toward the tree.

"No," Fred replied testily. "Are you here to shut her down? Shouldn't you be?"

"That's zoning," Jack replied. "I deal with abuse cases. I told you that when we spoke."

"She has dogs standing in filth."

"Not that I've seen and I've been here almost every day."

"They bark all night. Disturb the neighborhood."

"You have a zoning issue," Jack said. "There is no evidence of abuse here."

"Not now. You're probably in cahoots."

"Fred." Kat approached, frown etching her face. Behind her was Jack's family, a raven-colored poodle in Matthew's arms.

"Public events aren't allowed by the covenants," Fred said forcefully. He seemed agitated. "People are parked on the street as your lot isn't big enough."

"There is nothing illegal about parking on the street," Kat said.

"I have trouble driving down it. What if someone hits my car? This was a quiet neighborhood. Now there are dogs barking and . . . I have what I need. We'll be going."

The moment he and his friend shuffled out the door, Jack could see Kat deflating, the highs of her success replaced with Fred's low blow. So Jack said, "A poodle?"

In response, the dog in Matthew's arms barked. "Look Uncle Jack. I got a dog. Not one of those little ones either." He beamed from ear to ear.

"Please tell me you aren't going to put bows in its hair," Jack teased.

"He's a boy," Matthew announced. "Boy dogs don't have bows. Isn't he awesome?"

"Poodles are very loyal and don't shed much," Kat inserted the dog's merits before Jack could reply. "They are very smart and family oriented."

"And not that big," Sharon added.

"He's perfect," Matthew announced. "He's my Christmas present. I'm going to go tell Santa I have the one thing I really wanted."

"I'll take you over there," Joyce said, leading her grandson away. "We can take a picture." Matt's gaze trailed after them, before returning to Jack and Kat.

"So what was Fennewald doing here?" Jack's brother asked.

"Causing trouble," Kat said. Jack grabbed her hand for support. "But I wasn't going to cancel this event, even if Fred decides to sue me for this too. We've placed over half the animals. If they do shut me down, where would they have gone?"

"Well, we are quite pleased with our dog," Sharon said, changing the subject. "He's two and already trained.

What could be better? Let's go finish the paperwork. Matthew, that's a cute picture," Sharon called, heading toward Santa.

"Good luck," Matt said. "The guy with him is Kevin Banner. He's an ambulance chaser. Gives my profession a bad name." He followed his wife.

"You okay?" Jack asked Kat.

She sagged against him. "I'll just be glad when the case is over. One way or the other, at least I'll have some closure. Until then, there's nothing anyone can do, so let's get these animals into some good homes. You staying?"

Jack had at least twenty things he needed to do, things he hadn't managed to get done all week, like getting the oil in his car changed, getting his laundry done, getting his house cleaned. But only Kat mattered. Because they were at her workplace, he resisted the urge to kiss even her forehead, as he longed to do. "I'm staying."

His decision made those beautiful brown eyes brighten, and she perked up. He'd made her happy, and he liked that. Kat handed him a clipboard and an elf hat.

"That lovely couple right there has picked out brother and sister cats. We'd hoped to place them together and we have." She smiled at him and touched his arm, all the motivation he needed as it hinted at the promise of things to come. "I'll let you help them with their adoption paperwork."

He stared at the elf hat and the clipboard as she slipped away, recognizing the dare. He'd meet Kat's challenge, so he channeled his inner Will Ferrell, slid the green and yellow elf hat on his head, and waded in to help. He saw Kat only in passing the rest of the afternoon. The cookies his mom brought were long gone, as was most of the other food. He'd managed to snag three candy canes. His stomach rumbled as Kat finally locked the back door after the last of her employees left at five fifteen.

"What a day," she said. She wiped her forehead with the back of her wrist. "All but three. That's a new record."

"You had great publicity with Jingle being here."

"And you. Two hundred ten calendars. I didn't get enough."

He couldn't imagine signing more. "My mother bought twelve."

Kat began to laugh and covered her mouth. "Your mom is a hoot. You'll be everywhere, Mr. December."

"Don't you make fun of me," Jack said, grabbing her wrist and tugging her toward him. "It's not nice."

She flipped the pom-pom on his hat. "You deserved it. You didn't believe me about today."

"Maybe," he answered. "You did great. I stand corrected."

Her eyes twinkled and amusement edged the corners of her lips. "Say it."

"What? That you were an animal matchmaker?"

"You know what I want to hear. Say it."

He pulled her to him, her hands splaying against his chest. "What? You want to hear me grovel and say I was wrong?"

"You were, so yes, I do."

Jack didn't fully concede. "The jury's still out. As long as none of those animals come back."

"They won't," Kat declared.

Jack reached down to trace the blue stitching of her name. Her breath hitched.

"If they don't, then I will happily admit I was wrong. As it was, you talked my straightlaced, uptight brother into a full-size poodle. That's something I thought I'd never see. Matt with a dog."

"Fine. Close enough."

His fingers were at the top of her breast, mere inches from her nipple. Despite the lab coat and the clothes she wore underneath, heat pooled between her legs.

"Why is the writing always blue?"

"I don't know."

"Katherine with a K. " His voice dropped and he outlined the first letter again.

"My grandmother's name. I shortened it to Kat one day because I couldn't spell it all. I was four."

"Precocious."

He finger rubbed over the letters and she toyed with a button on his shirt. "You're just jealous Jack isn't short for anything."

"Ha. Is too. Jackson. Jackson Howard."

She giggled. "Howard."

"Don't mock my grandpa. He's a great guy."

She popped open the button. "I'm not. I'm making fun of you."

"That's not nice. You know, you're not being very nice

to me. You made me wear this hat."

"It looked sexy in the calendar."

"That was a Santa hat."

"Close enough." Her breath hitched. "And now you're toying with me."

He tugged her closer to him so that her hands flattened between them. "You're the tease. Not me."

"Me?" Kat parroted innocently. "How?"

"Just, just everything. You are driving me absolutely crazy."

She leaned her head back, brought her face upward. "So? What are you going to do about it?"

"This," Jack replied, and swallowed her next words with a kiss that left her knees wobbly. His tongue found crevices in her mouth that she didn't know could emit such pleasure. She dragged her teeth along his tongue, and he groaned. "You are so tempting."

"Really?" Her mouth kissed the edge of his.

He stepped back. "If we don't get out of here, this will get out of hand. Dinner."

Reluctantly, Kat agreed. Before her employees had left, all the animals had been fed and taken care of, including Jingle. She could leave work, go to dinner. "I need my purse. It's in my office."

He entered her office. She bent down to retrieve her purse from the locked drawer but Jack was right behind her, and he put his hands on her bottom and then slid them around to pull her back toward his groin.

"You are so sexy," he told her. Rather than straighten,

Kat parted her legs so his hands could slide between. She and Jack had been building to this moment, and she wanted it. She wanted sparks. Wanted heat. He ground her into him and she gasped as his left hand came up to pull out her shirt and move underneath to cup her breast. "So damn hot," Jack said. He lowered his lips to her neck.

Kat's brain short-circuited. No way could she go eat dinner in this aroused state. Her breast fell heavy in his left hand and his right hand moved between her legs, the black chinos a barrier to full friction.

"Jack."

He drew back. "I know. Not romantic. I'm taking you to dinner now. I'm sorry . . ."

"I'm not." She faced him, grabbed his shirt, pushed him back toward the couch. The back of his knees connected with it, and he sat. She straddled him, brought her mouth close to his. She'd never been this brazen before, but she wanted him. "I know you're a decent, upright guy who always does the right thing. Now shut up and kiss me."

He obliged, capturing her lips and sliding his tongue deep. His fingers found the buttons of her shirt, and soon it and the lab coat were on the floor. She wore red lace, and Jack peeled it low, exposing her breasts. He captured one and swirled his tongue over it, making Kat cry out in pleasure.

"Sensitive."

"Oh yes," she said, kissing his neck and inhaling the musky scent so uniquely him.

"Good?" He moved to the other breast.

"Hell yes," Kat moaned as her body quaked. "Don't you dare stop."

"A gentleman—"

"Would meet all my needs."

"Then I'm going to make you come all night," he told her.

"Oh!" She shattered as fingers and tongue worked their magic.

"One," Jack counted. He grinned at her. "And so you know, I always keep my promises."

He undid her belt and top button, tugging the zipper free so he could dip a finger inside her pants. He made a circle and she cried out. He slid under the red lace she wore and stroked from top to bottom, before adding another finger. Then he slid both inside her moist heat, and Kat shouted with the ecstasy.

"That's right. Come for me," he told her as he placed his mouth on her nipple, bringing her to orgasm again as she rode his fingers.

Kat's head rolled onto his shoulder. Never before had an orgasm been so satisfying—and she could tell they weren't finished. Jack licked his fingers and closed his eyes as he tasted her. "You are delicious. So sweet."

"Oh." But she lost words as he stripped her of her pants, leaving her only in red lace bra and undies. Then he turned her so her back was on the couch and he knelt on the floor and pushed her legs apart. "Lady in red," he whispered as he lowered his mouth to her throbbing, wet center. The fabric provided a seductive texture until Jack pushed the lace aside so his tongue could taste her unimpeded. Kat could only watch through half-lidded eyes as that gorgeous blond man drank her in. Blue eyes locked on hers as he slid one finger, then two, back inside, his kisses causing her to throw her head back and let go as the world shook yet again.

"You are soaked," he told her as he stood, stripping his clothes, and Kat reached to check, if only to desensitize her pulsating flesh. He pushed her hand away. "My job. You need something to hold. Here."

He stood long, thick, and hard, barely fitting in her hand. Beautiful. Then Kat got greedy and wrapped her mouth around him. He groaned. "I wasn't meaning you had to do that."

"Shut up," she told him, for she needed to regain some control, some female power after being shattered so thoroughly. She cupped him, took him as deep into her mouth as she could until he was drawing back, sliding her to the edge of the couch, and turning her body so he could enter her. He managed get the condom on in record time before driving himself inside in one, blissful, earth-shattering thrust.

Kat wrapped one leg around him, the other on the floor as he stroked, and she heard herself making all those embarrassing noises she hated but couldn't check as pleasure overtook reason. Then she didn't care, for she saw stars and every nerve ending overloaded and quaked. He used his fingers and rubbed her as well, and his lips came down to kiss her breast, his tongue circling her nipple.

He increased his pace and the orgasm of all orgasms overtook her, sending her into the place where the mind goes blank and only pure pleasure existed. She was floating, riding a wave, and suddenly, as she felt him pulse, her whole body shook and she erupted and was spent. Sweat beaded his brow and she wiped it off before bringing him close. "Damn."

"Uh-huh," she agreed. *Best sex ever. And the night was young.*

They stayed quiet, each touching the other softly as their bodies calmed. His stomach rumbled. "I missed lunch," he told her.

"You didn't grab any of the sandwiches?"

"Got busy." He drew back, touched her breast. "Would rather stay busy."

"Hmmm. Then luckily the Chinese place delivers. My flat's closer and besides, the night tech comes in at seven."

Jack shifted. "Then we'll need to go so we can continue this."

"After all, you made a promise," Kat teased.

"That I did," he said with a grin that twisted something inside her heart. "And I always keep my promises. So let's get out of here."

Chapter Ten

Jack woke up to the realization he wasn't alone. He was on his back, with Kat curled to the left side of him. But when he opened his eyes, the first thing he saw was the white and brown face with whiskers a mere six inches from his chin. Pippa had planted herself in the middle of his chest. Luckily there was a sheet between her paws and his bare chest.

Jack tilted his head, seeing Ty sleeping at the foot of the bed. Unlike him, Kat always had company, albeit the pet variety.

"What time is it?" Kat mumbled sleepily. She rolled over, her naked rear sliding away from where it had been pressed against his hip. Now her chest came to rest beside his, those beautiful breasts rubbing against him. Part of him stirred, although the last time they'd joined had been mere hours. How much sleep had they even gotten?

Pippa dug in her claws as Jack shifted to see the clock. The sheet did little to protect. "Ouch!"

Kat rose up, her naked torso glorious as she picked up the kitten and relocated her to another part of the bed. Jack leaned over to catch a nipple with his mouth, and Kat arched her back as he drew the nub between his lips.

"You are dangerous," she said.

"Mmm hmm," he murmured, his hand already reaching for her core. He was rock hard; and he had a hunch she was already wet for him. He drew her on top of him, and she slid down. He loved how he fit inside her so perfectly, and he captured her breast fully as she began to ride him. He allowed her to set the pace until he knew she was close, and then he put his hands on her hips to keep her moving as her body joined his in the release both sought.

He'd never had sex so good, so perfect. So mind blowing. He wasn't sure he could ever get enough of Kat.

They ate a late breakfast around noon, after a long shower. Kat scrambled some eggs, and he scarfed down the entire plate.

"You're hungry."

"We didn't eat much of that Chinese," Jack reminded her. Who needed food when there was Kat?

Kat blushed. Jack now knew that pinkish color went head to toe. "We were otherwise occupied," Kat said.

"I'd say," Jack replied. Her hair was loose around her shoulders and she wore a tank top and those yoga pants. She was beautiful.

"So do you have a busy week?" she asked.

"Have to pick up my tux Wednesday. There's some

groomsmen dinner thing on Tuesday."

"What about the bachelor party?"

"A few weeks ago. More like a dinner at a sports bar. Matt and I both skipped the after-party. Brian's only twenty-two, and we just didn't feel comfortable heading over to the east side and the strip clubs. Something he and I agreed on, amazingly enough."

"It doesn't seem like you are your brother are close."

"Depends on the day. Most days I'm a bit of a disappointment."

Having no siblings, she didn't quite know how to respond. "I'm sorry to hear that. You'll have to let me know how the puppy fared."

Jack picked up his phone. Amazingly the damn thing had been silent. Not one call or text. He put it back on the kitchen table. "Will do. You know Sharon's going to put bows in that dog's hair."

"Dogs don't have gender issues. People do."

Jack and Kat both laughed. "True. So what's your week look like?"

"Just patients. Same old thing."

"Would you like to do something?"

"When?"

"How about now? I could run home, change, pick you up in an hour. We could go to Forest Park." Ideas came to him. "The History Museum. Art Museum. Ice skating."

"Ice skating?"

"Should be an afternoon public session at Steinberg, and it's been cold enough."

"We can stay indoors," Kat said, for Steinberg was an outdoor rink. Although, she appreciated Jack's efforts. "There might even be a Blues game. That's a good compromise. We can *watch* skating."

"Let me check." Jack slid his finger over his phone and did a quick search. "There is. Shall we go?"

"As in a real date?" She had to know.

Jack tilted his head, considered. "I don't know what the rules are for this anymore"—he gestured aimlessly—"especially after last night. I like being with you. I'd like to get to know you better. But—"

"I know. You don't have a good track record and you can't commit. I didn't forget." She checked her disappointment. She'd hoped last night might have changed things. Once again she'd let her emotions overrule logic, had jumped in without thinking. "When's the game?"

"Six."

"Then we have plenty of time. You could help me with my Christmas shopping," she teased, knowing clear well he'd say no.

"I avoid malls like the plague, especially in December."

Just as she'd predicted. "Actually, I want to go to Cherokee Street. I'm looking for something specific and didn't find it when they had their cookie walk."

The antique district held an annual cookie walk the first weekend of December—each shop put out trays of cookies to entice shoppers.

"We can do that," Jack said.

Surprise had her staring at him. "Really? You'd shop with me?"

He'd spend time with her any way he could. "Sure. Then dinner and the Blues game."

Kat walked him to the back door. He'd parked behind her garage. "One hour," he told her as he kissed her. "Not a second more."

"Yes sir," she quipped, tearing her lips from his and shutting the door behind him. She watched him walk across her backyard and waited until the SUV drove away. Then she raced to get ready. In the spirit of Christmas, Kat wasn't going to question this gift.

***

Little more than an hour later, Kat and Jack strolled down Cherokee Street. Known for its antique shops, streetlights sported Christmas wreaths and trees contained strands of lights. They ducked under the green awning and through the heavy wooden front door of Hammond Books, a vintage bookstore with shelves crammed together so tightly that Jack bumped into Kat every turn. Not that he minded being close.

"I love this place," she said, browsing through the books on the first floor for fifteen minutes before heading up the narrow back stairs to thumb through vintage posters.

"Well, Barnes and Noble doesn't have a chandelier."

"That it doesn't," Kat said, finding a biography that caught her interest. "My dad would like this. He has one of those old-fashioned libraries, complete with a window seat. I would curl up and read for hours."

"No library in our house. We were packed in pretty tight. I walked to the nearby library. Quieter there. Where'd you live?"

"I grew up in Clayton. On Southmoor."

Jack knew the area. Big houses. Lots of land. Expensive. "So did you go to Clayton?"

"MICDS." Kat named one of St. Louis's premier private high schools as she spotted a crystal necklace at the counter.

"Ah."

"Don't make me out for a snob. Just because St. Louis is all about where you went to high school doesn't mean I fit the stereotype. I loved science, and have you seen the science building?"

Jack held up his hands, conceding the point. She spotted a display of jewelry. "Pretty. And only twenty-five dollars. My cousin will like this." She purchased that and the book, and then they walked west several blocks to China Finders, where Kat found a set of cat bookends she had to have. "For my partner's wife," she told Jack, who took the paper bag that he knew would get heavier the longer he toted it.

"Cupcake?" she suggested, and they crossed Missouri Avenue and went through the blue double doors into Whisk. The bakery was an overload of Christmas decorations, and Kat and Jack checked the chalkboard of the day's specials before opting instead for banana chocolate-chip muffins and coffee. They sat near the front windows so they could watch the passersby. Kat enjoyed the easy companionship she found with Jack.

"So what else do you need to find?"

"I think I'm good," Kat said. She glanced at her watch. The day had flown by. "How about you? Have you bought all your presents?"

"I do gift cards."

"Jack!"

He didn't appear sheepish. "What else do you get someone who has everything?"

"It's so impersonal. Your mother is a lovely woman. She'd probably love a scarf. Or we saw those lovely ceramic Christmas trees. I'm sure she could find a home for those."

"She had every inch of the house covered."

"So do I. She can find room."

"I don't get it. What is it with decorating? I don't even have a tree."

"No tree?"

"It's just me. Why do I need one? And go ahead and say it. Everyone else does. I'm a Scrooge."

"I don't like to call out names. How long have you been doing gift cards?"

Jack thought back. "Since they became fashionable?"

"That's terrible."

"Not really. When we were little, Matt and I always competed for who would get Mom the best gift. He always won."

"I'm sure he didn't."

"He bragged he did."

"Jack, she's your mom." Kat had sudden insight into the boy he must have been, suddenly thrust from the one caring for his mother to the one having to share her with a new family. "You were never less in her eyes. You couldn't have been."

"He's the golden boy. I'm the black sheep. Easier to play the role."

Kat shook her head and reached for his hand. "Oh, Jack. I'm not going to assume I can give you advice, especially as I have no siblings."

"And I'll thank you for that. You won't believe how many women think they can fix me. Blending families is hard," Jack admitted. "We can leave it at that."

"I don't think you need fixing. A Christmas tree, perhaps, but no fixing."

An eyebrow arched. "No?"

"I'm not that presumptuous. If you can't accept a person how he or she is, then you shouldn't be with that person." She paused. "I learned that the hard way. College boyfriend. Didn't like all my long hours. Wanted me to be a stay-at-home mom and not even pursue opening a clinic. I wasted quite a few years until I wised up and realized there was nothing wrong with him except that he was wrong for me."

"I can understand that," Jack replied. "You spend a lot of years in complacency and mediocrity because it's easier than facing the world by yourself."

"Twenties suck. I'm glad to be almost out of them."

"So you're not going to get on my case about buying a tree?"

She shook her head. "No. You'll get one when you're ready."

They'd finished their drinks and returned the mugs to the washtub.

"You still up for hockey?" Jack asked. He held her bags in one hand and reached with the other.

Kat grinned. "You bet."

"Then let's go."

By the end of the evening, as Jack walked her to her back door, Kat realized she was smiling that goofy grin a woman gets when she's happy. The Blues had defeated the L.A. Kings by three, and she and Jack had been behind the Blues bench, in the top part of Section 103 where they'd had a great view of the action. He draped an arm around her.

"You want to come up?"

"Just to carry these up," Jack replied. He followed her up the back stairs and set her packages inside on the kitchen table. Immediately Pippa and Ty vied for her attention.

"See, if you get any pets, they'll greet you when you get home," she said.

He picked up Pippa, who flopped into his arms and sprawled out, stomach up. "Look how loose she is."

"I know. She's like jello. I've never had a cat who did

171

that before."

"I had a good time today," Jack said suddenly. "Thanks for going."

"So did I help reinvigorate your holiday spirit?" Kat teased.

"Maybe a little," Jack admitted. He scratched Pippa's head, and the kitten closed her eyes and began to purr. "She's a sweetheart. So are you." He kept the cat between them like a shield. "Where do we go from here?"

"I don't know. What do you want?" Kat asked.

I want you. The words came from his core and shook his very foundation. "I don't want us to get hurt."

"Then let's keep playing things by ear. As long as we promise to be honest with each other, then we should be fine."

"You really believe that?"

Kat wasn't one hundred percent sure, but she knew for certain she didn't want Jack walking out the kitchen door. "Yes. So why don't you put Pippa down and kiss me?"

He grinned, let the cat go. Pippa dropped gently to the floor and headed for her food dish. "When did you become so bossy and demanding?"

"Probably once Mr. December first seduced me."

"Oh. Well, he wasn't wearing a Santa hat."

Kat grabbed Jack and drew him to her for a long kiss. "Don't worry," she told him. "That can be arranged."

***

Six days later, Kat sat in the second row pew, right behind Jack's parents and grandparents, crammed between aunts, uncles, cousins, and other miscellaneous family members. Kat had met Jack's stepfather's parents and his maternal grandparents at last night's rehearsal dinner, along with younger sister Brenna.

She and Sharon were in the wedding, along with Jack and Matt who stood beside Brian, Cecily's fiancé. They weren't alone—sixteen total attendants were gathered at the front of the church, and that wasn't even counting the couple getting married or the priest.

The groomsmen had helped seat attendees, so Jack had escorted Kat to her seat. She'd worn a dark green A-line velvet dress that ended right below her knees. The scoop bodice hugged the tops of her breasts without being revealing, and the dress had cute cap sleeves. She'd bought it Wednesday night, wanting something different yet in the Christmas spirit.

"Isn't this wonderful?" an older woman seated next to her whispered as the music began and the wedding party came down the aisle.

"Yes," Kat replied, turning her head to try to see through all the columns and down the long center aisle. At least she wasn't in one of the side sections.

Of the eight groomsmen, Jack came down the aisle fifth. He escorted a good friend of Cecily's, whom Kat had met last night after she'd watched this whole ritual being rehearsed. As Jack approached, a lump formed in Kat's throat. She'd seen him twice in a tux, but perhaps it was the magic of weddings, for he was more handsome, more desirable than ever. He searched her out, and as their gaze connected, he gave her a conspiratorial wink. Her heart jumped.

Then he stood up front, and she couldn't help but flush under his intense gaze. Then another groomsman crossed in front and another, diverting Jack's attention.

She rose with the crowd when the bride arrived, sat back down as the ceremony began.

The wedding was gorgeous. Last night the priest had done a lot of "then we say vows and then you walk to the statute of Mary over there and . . ." and while people moved about, the Thursday night rehearsal hadn't held the enchanted quality of the actual service.

"Hey," Jack said, coming back up the side aisle and entering her pew. She was the only person left, the relatives to her right having walked to the front so they could greet family and friends.

"Beautiful ceremony," she said. They stepped out into the aisle.

"Long. Thought Cecily and Brian would never get that unity candle to light. Is it hot in here?" Jack tugged at his tie; she knew how much he hated them. She reached up, adjusted the black bow. "Thought they might burn the place down."

Kat stifled a giggle and glanced furtively at the family members who stood nearby. Hopefully they hadn't overheard. "Shh. People are listening."

He gave a nonchalant shrug and that little grin she

liked, the one he often shot her as he traced her belly button with his fingertip. "Ah, I'm the black sheep. Nothing new. It'll just give them something else to talk about, keep the gossips happy."

"Jack." A petite white-haired woman gave him a big hug as she passed by.

"That's Aunt Rachel. We're going to have at least a half hour of photos, maybe more as my family takes forever. How about you meet me at the reception? I'll catch a ride with my parents."

"You sure?"

"I'd be the first one out the door if I could," Jack admitted. "But Cecily would shoot me and my mother would stomp on my bullet-riddled carcass."

Kat burst out laughing. Having met his mother, she agreed. "I just bet that's what would happen."

"So, as I love both of them and value my life, I'm going to smile wide and keep my mouth shut."

He leaned over, his exhale hot in her ear. "I also want to make love to you later tonight, and I need to be very alive for that."

His voice caressed over her, and she gave an anticipatory shiver. "Sounds like a good plan then."

"Definitely." He touched her arm, creating the automatic tingles that filled her with longing. "Get going. I've already done all the groom shots, thank God." He held out his car keys and tilted his head. "Besides, if you stay, my mom's going to try to put you in all the family photos."

The keys warmed in her hand, and she tried to keep

things light. "Reception sounds grand. Besides, there's wine there."

"That there is. Lucky you." Jack gave her a lingering kiss on the lips.

"You next down the aisle, Jack?" someone called. "This is a church you know. Show some respect or finally get the deed done yourself."

He drew away, running a forefinger down her cheek. "There are moments I hate my family."

"Well, don't kill that person," Kat warned, trying to keep from laughing while at the same time willing her body not to react to his brief touch. All he had to do now was look at her and she'd ignite. "Your sister won't like it."

"Jack! Photos!" someone called.

Jack exhaled and rolled his eyes. "See you in a few, or hopefully before I'm old and gray."

"I'll have a beer waiting."

He kissed her lips lightly before moving away. "You are definitely a goddess. An angel."

"Don't you forget it," Kat called after him, a soft, fuzzy feeling blooming. She put on her dress coat, then drove Jack's SUV less than five minutes away to the South Side institution called Hendri's. Kat stepped into the banquet hall and stopped short, as if frozen. She frowned, willing her feet to move. Was she glued down?

She turned her head, taking in the view before her. The room was perfect. Round eight-top tables covered with white tablecloths were interspersed between similarly covered rectangular tables that sat ten. Chairs were covered with solid-black fabric, complete with white bows on the back. White rose centerpieces with plaid bows sat on the center of each table. Hendri's even had a black-and-white diamond-patterned dance floor.

Her feet still didn't move. Then it hit her. She wanted this. *A wedding. A reception. A family.*

She wanted it all. She'd thought she'd have a happily-ever-after with her ex, Rick, but when she'd gone to vet school, they'd fallen apart in a brutal, self-esteem-killing way. So she'd buried this particular dream deep inside, for it was easier to ignore what you knew you couldn't have rather than try to find another way to get it.

People moved around her, and Kat realized she was blocking the middle of the doorway. She jolted into action, finding the name card that told her where she sat. She set her purse on her chair and noticed a small crowd gathered at the long, dark-wood bar. It reminded her of something she'd seen in Irish pub, or one of those familiar neighborhood places that have been around forever. Kat joined the queue as more revelers arrived.

"Riesling and a Bud," she told the bartender, who with practiced efficiency filled a wineglass and handed her a longneck. Kat took a sip of wine as she stood there. St. Louis was the type of place where you'd always run into someone you knew. At a Blues game, she'd find herself on the one escalator where at the top she'd run into her college roommate's friend Jose, the arena's head of security. Walk into any restaurant, she'd often run into a client.

Tonight Kat didn't recognize a soul. So she did what

every other single person does when faced with awkward circumstances: return to the table, pull out her cell phone, and check her Facebook status and e-mail.

Thankfully Jack arrived within a half hour; he dropped into the seat next to her, grabbed his still somewhat cold beer, and took a long swallow. "Needed this."

"That answers how photos went."

"If my mother wasn't in the photographs, she would have been taking them herself. As it is, she micromanaged that guy within an inch of his life. Speak of the devil. . ." His voice trailed off as Joyce approached, and he stood and kissed her cheek. "Mom."

With a nod at Jack, Joyce reached for Kat's hands. Her silvery beaded gown caught the light. "Kat! So good to see you again. Didn't you just love the wedding?" She gave Kat's hands a little squeeze.

"It was beautiful." Kat pulled her hands back and put them in her lap. Joyce remained standing, so Kat tilted her head back.

"It was. I'm so glad you're here. Jack's seated over there."

"I'd rather be over here."

Joyce smiled widely "Too bad. And you know what they say, absence makes the heart fonder."

Jack groaned as his mother tugged his arm. "That's my cue." He gave Kat a parting kiss. "Good luck."

Kat found herself surround by some of the same people with whom she'd been placed in the church pew. Dinner was a buffet of roast beef, chicken marsala, rigatoni pasta with a choice of white or red sauces, mixed green salad, and a broccoli, cauliflower and carrot mix. Afterward came speeches, cake cutting, and finally the bride and groom's first dance.

Then Jack found Kat, sans bow tie, and told her, "I'm free." He pulled her out onto the dance floor, where they showed off their moves until a slow song began. Then he drew her to him, her head resting on his chest. He smelled divine.

"I like having you in my arms," Jack whispered.

"I like being here," Kat said, snuggling closer as they swayed to the music for two songs. She fit in his arms like she'd been made for him. She'd never been so at ease or comfortable. Jack made her feel special. She just had to remember to take tomorrow one day at a time, as cliché as that sounded.

They broke apart after the DJ told everyone it was time for the father/daughter dance. While everyone waited for Nelson and Cecily to take the floor, Kat headed for the bathroom; Jack went to the bar. "Just water," she called. "Dehydrated."

The room was empty when she entered, but as she was washing her hands a young woman approached and caught her eye through the mirror. Kat smiled at her because that's what you did at weddings.

"So you're the wedding date."

Kat's smile faded slightly, but she didn't falter. "I am Jack's date," she corrected, tone pleasant.

The woman turned her face, checking her makeup.

Then she zeroed in on Kat again. "How long have you been dating?"

"Since the end of November," Kat replied.

"Not very long at all."

An uneasy feeling grew in the pit of Kat's stomach. "Long enough that he chose to bring me to this and the rehearsal."

The platinum blond refreshed blood-red lipstick, her green gaze assessing. Her lips made an annoying pop as she pressed them together, puckered, and released. "Well, I hope you aren't hoping for a commitment. I went to two or three of these things with Jack and it didn't budge him an inch." She redid her bottom lip with a swipe, a large diamond on her ring finger flashing. She made the annoying pop again. "Some men are like that."

Kat bristled. "Like what? Wise?"

The blond had the audacity to laugh. "Oh honey, *I* dumped *him*."

"And I can reassure you he's grateful for that fact every day," Kat replied, head high as she left the bathroom before she let her claws fully come out. She didn't get far before being cornered by Sharon, who winced as she saw the woman leave the bathroom a few seconds after Kat.

"I saw her heading your way. I came as fast as I could. Sorry I didn't get in there in time."

Kat's glance trailed the annoying blond. "Who was that?"

"Julie. The ex."

The five-year ex. Jack's long-term girlfriend. The one

he'd refused to marry after she'd given an ultimatum. "She . . . wasn't very nice," Kat burst out before she could stop herself. "What other type of woman has the nerve to approach me in the bathroom to give me a lecture on Jack's lack of commitment?" Kat relayed the entire conversation.

"Oh that's priceless. I wish I could have seen her face." Sharon waved her hand in front of her mouth as if that would somehow stop her immediate laughter. "Truer words were never spoken. She is a bitch. None of us want her here, but she's engaged to one of Brian's friends. We were never her biggest fans. She wasn't right for Jack. Not the way you are."

Kat let that latter part slide. "I just wish Jack would have told me she was coming."

"I doubt he knew. He did his job and showed up in a tux, which is about all you can expect from Jack when it comes to weddings. They make him uncomfortable. Maybe it has to do with holidays. I don't think he is in to all of the pomp and circumstance. I'm sure some psychoanalyst could have a field day with him. Oops, shouldn't have said that. Now I'm going to scare you away. Believe me, there is no person more loyal and loving than Jack. When family needs him, he's there one hundred ten percent."

"It's fine," Kat mumbled, absorbing.

The two women made their way back into the main room, where the single women were lining up for Cecily's bouquet toss. "Get in there," Joyce urged, snagging Kat mere seconds through the archway.

"But I—" Kat protested. However, Joyce propelled Kat by the elbow until she stood next to Brenna in the middle of the crowd.

"I see my mom got you here too," Brenna said with a whimsical laugh. "I'm nineteen. As if. Dumb tradition."

"Well, I don't want it. I'm not even sure why I'm here . . ." Kat was not paying any attention as the throwaway bouquet hit her smack dab in the face. Her hands instinctively went to protect herself, and she caught the roses perfectly. "Damn it." She plastered on a smile and held the flowers high as, all around her, people applauded.

Joyce materialized. "A picture, Kat," she insisted, the beleaguered photographer trailing behind. "Cecily said she might get them to you and she did. Oh, I do hope you're next. You are perfect for Jack! You really keep him in line, and he's been so much happier lately. I can't wait until the day I can welcome you to the family properly."

"I'm not, we're not . . ." Kat said, but Joyce gushed on and Kat tuned her out. Across the room, Jack smiled and raised his beer in a toast. He'd managed to wiggle out of the garter toss. "Smile dear," Joyce said, and Kat smiled automatically for the camera.

Joyce gave her hands a squeeze. "You are so good for my son. Look at him smiling!

But she wasn't smiling, and that fact sat heavy, was almost oppressive. Around her, people had the time of their lives and the bride and groom got ready to spend their first night as husband and wife. Kat made a beeline for Jack the moment the photographer said "Thanks" and Joyce let her go. She hated tearing Jack away from his sister's reception, but she couldn't stay another minute.

"I need you to take me home."

He blinked, his smile fading. "Huh?"

"I'm not feeling well. I want to go home now," she told him. Her words came out harsher than expected, so she tempered them. "I'm tired. Long day at the office and I ate way too much. I hope I'm not coming down with anything. You can just take me home and drop me off. Come right back."

Worry creased his brow. "Then I'll get our coats."

Jack headed off as Kat stood by her table and sipped the cup of water he'd gotten for her.

"You leaving?" Joyce asked, frown on her face.

Kat nodded as something inside her fisted tight. She wasn't lying as she replied, "I am. I'm not feeling well and I worked all day. Jack will come right back."

"He should stay with you." Joyce put her hand on Kat's forehead. "You don't feel warm. I hope you're okay. Will we see you Sunday night for dinner?"

"I don't think so," Kat replied, as the truth became a bitter pill. She couldn't allow herself to become involved any deeper. Jack's family consisted of wonderful people, but as much as she liked them, she didn't belong here. She couldn't keep letting them think this was real. She couldn't continue the charade another minute more. If she kept pretending, she'd be in a lie she'd never let end. Her heart belonged to Jack, and tonight proved she wanted her own wedding. However, Jack had repeatedly told her he wasn't looking for commitment.

"But we would love to see you Sunday and—"

Kat grabbed Joyce's hands as Joyce had done so many times to her. "We'll catch up later," she fibbed because doing so was easier. Then she strode to the coat check, where Jack stood with a deep, forehead-creasing frown.

"What's wrong?" he asked as they drove away. "Did I do something to upset you? Or was it Julie? I saw her and—"

"No, it wasn't Julie. It's me."

Her apartment was ten minutes away. Time to get this over with, run inside, lick her wounds, and hide until tomorrow. "I think we should call this off. We're lying to everyone and I can't do it anymore."

She saw only his vague profile inside the darkened car. Silence fell, and she rushed to fill the noiseless vacuum. "The wedding's over. If we stage a breakup, then your family will be off your back for the holidays, and we don't have to pretend anymore."

"This night didn't feel like pretending, Kat. I thought we agreed we were comfortable taking things as they arrived."

"All we've done is have sex. We don't have a real relationship. We have something else. I'm not exactly sure what to call it." Kat knew she wasn't making sense. She'd never been good at articulating her feelings, especially under this kind of pressure. "The bottom line is this—us— isn't going anywhere. We're having a good time, but . . ."

"There's always a but."

"I'm not going to be your ex. I'm not going to issue an ultimatum. Better we end it now rather than later, when your family thinks we're too involved. Or when we hate each other. Or when your family expects you to marry me, as clearly they do as your sister deliberately hit me in the face with her flowers. She's not that bad of an aim."

"What if I don't want this to end? Does what I want count?"

She sighed. You couldn't change what had never truly been real. "Jack, from the moment I met you, you said no commitment. Trust me. It's better this way. Much better. Besides, I have my court case Monday. I need to focus on that. This has all been one big distraction. I've let myself pretend, believe things I shouldn't have. Besides, my lawyer says our relationship might have even made things worse."

"I don't believe that. What we have is special. We should talk this out. Work something out."

"Like what?"

"I don't know," he admitted, fingers tight on the steering wheel. "Just know that I've never wanted to work things out with anyone else before. It's never felt right before, which is why I've hesitated."

"It doesn't matter." Kat hated how cruel her words sounded. "It's my life. It's what I believe that matters. It's better if we don't see each other anymore. Go back to maintaining our professional distance."

They'd reached her apartment, and he drove into the back alley. She wanted to touch him, take away the pain she could see written on his face, pain she'd caused.

Oh God, she was head-over-heels in love with him. She'd fallen hard, fast, and deep for a man who could never love her back.

Like all those Christmas movies, she'd bought into the fantasy, the fairy tale, the belief that things would work out. Her own warning returned to haunt her.

She tossed open the car door, but he was there in an instant to help her out. He touched her arm, and her skin caught fire through the fabric. *God, even after all of that she still wanted him!* "Don't do this."

"I can't keep living a lie," she said, her heart breaking. Sharp stabbing pieces knifed inside her chest. She'd found the perfect man for her—only his work came first. She understood that, but boy did she want to change it.

"Kat—" Jack began. He reached for her, but Kat backed away. How easy it would be to cave, to say yes, to take him into her arms and whisk him upstairs. She could lose herself in the lovemaking that always made her resplendent and complete. Say yes, and she wouldn't be alone at Christmas, wouldn't be alone on New Year's.

But tonight's wedding revealed that she wanted it all and that she would rather have nothing than settle for something in between that would never provide true fulfillment, something that would always keep her hoping and wishing for more. Jack had dated Julie for five years. Kat was merely a month. She'd chosen the wrong man to love, but part of her wanted to continue blithely along. All she had to do was say yes, let's talk. She'd learned hope was for the naïve and foolish. Time to fully grow up.

"I can't," she said, and then she turned and fled.

#

Jack stood there in the bone-numbing December cold and watched the lights flicker on one by one in Kat's apartment before he climbed into his car and started the engine. He sat there stunned. *What the hell had happened? Everything had been so amazing and then . . .*

He shivered, the despair building inside of him leaving him dumbfounded and angry. How did that song go, "You don't know what you have until you let it go"?

Emotions he'd long buried roared forward, his internal voice yelling, "You fool. You did it again."

He'd just watched the future he hadn't known he wanted disappear two flights up, into a two-family building covered with an overdose of Christmas lights. When had the holiday become so disillusioning? When had he simply lost the Christmas spirit? When had he become his own worst enemy?

He'd discovered joy again. He'd found Kat's holiday enthusiasm contagious. For the first time in years, he hadn't dreaded the holidays and his well-meaning but overbearing family. She'd also tempered his cynicism. Her passion for animals was stellar; her love complete. Why hadn't he seen what was right in front of him? She'd thawed that part inside of him he'd kept frozen, kept safe. No guy wanted to be hurt again.

So he'd become a man stuck in his ways. He'd hidden behind a mask—he was too busy with work to date.

Reality had a way of smacking the crap out of a

person, Jack thought bitterly. Like an ugly blow upside the head, he'd learned too late. He no longer wanted to play pretend with Kat, but he'd never told her he'd changed his mind and wanted things to be real. He'd only reinforced his lack of commitment in their relationship. He tasted the word, rolled it over his tongue. Found it didn't scare him anymore, not where Kat was concerned. As Cecily had said, when you know, you know. *He loved Kat.*

Sitting in his car, he suddenly knew what he wanted. He'd played house long enough with Julie to know when something wasn't working, but inertia meant he'd simply abided her presence until she'd given him an ultimatum and walked away. Yeah, that made him a lousy guy. Tack on his failures with Kat, and he was batting a thousand in the "I suck" relationship department.

He blasted the heater. He didn't want to go home, not to the bed she'd shared. Not to the Christmas tree he'd purchased the day after the Blues game so he'd have something Christmassy in his apartment when she visited. He had to do something. With a deep, fortifying breath, he knew he needed to man up and go see the one person he needed the most.

"Mom," he said as he walked back into the reception hall. The party was still in full swing.

"Jack." Concern laced her face as she rushed over. "How is Kat? The poor dear."

"She called it off. She and I. We're done."

Stunned, Joyce dropped into the closest chair, her silvery dress fanning out. "What?"

Jack sat beside her, the black chair covering sliding loose under his legs. "It's my fault. We—I—Oh hell. It wasn't real."

His mom appeared confused. Eyes so like his blinked rapid fire. "What wasn't real? You and Kat? How can that be?"

"We made it all up."

"Jack."

"I know. I'm a heel. A lousy son. I'm . . ." He raked a hand through his hair.

"She cares for you, and you her. But before you continue, I think your stepfather should hear this too."

"You're probably right," Jack agreed. Might as well face it all at once.

She waved Jack's stepfather over, and Jack stretched his legs out as Nelson sat next to his wife. "Tell us what is going on," Joyce demanded, tone eerily calm. "The whole truth."

Jack took a deep breath, akin to those he'd taken before confessing he'd been the one who'd broken the lamp or the kitchen window. Those now seemed like cake compared to this.

"I asked Kat to pretend to date me so you'd get off my back about one, a wedding date, and two, my lack of relationships." He winced. That sounded really bad, and his mother's wounded expression said it all.

"This is my fault?" his mom asked.

"No, mine. One hundred percent," Jack admitted. "You do like to meddle with relationships, but I should have been honest with you. I know that. Now." He chewed his lip. "I've botched this with Kat from the very beginning. We did meet when she saved Jingle, but we'd met earlier at the calendar ball and shared a moment and then she was gone. Then I saw her save Jingle and . . . it went from there. We came up with a scheme. It was a dumb idea."

"How do you feel about her?"

"I'm not sure," Jack said, not ready to admit aloud that he loved her. The words he'd thought in the car were still too new to voice to someone else. Kat deserved to hear them first.

"I think you *are* sure," his stepfather pointed out. "Son, it sounds like she might be the one."

"She is the one," Joyce announced with annoying certainty. "But Jack's late to the table in figuring that out. Well, one thing's for sure, you have to win her back. What are you planning to do to fix this? Groveling helps."

Jack shook his head, remembering all those long talks he and Kat had had wee into the morning. "I'm a workaholic like her parents. I'm the wrong guy. She needs someone stable. Someone who will be there for her."

"How is that not you?" Joyce demanded. "When did you become such a quitter?"

Sharon and Matt approached. "Are we missing a family meeting?" Matt asked.

"Jack screwed it up with Kat," Joyce announced. Jack's fists tightened.

"But I like her," Sharon said. "She put Julie in her

place tonight like nothing I've ever seen." Sharon relayed the story.

"That girl has gumption," Nelson announced, and Jack heard the awe in his voice. "Enough to stand up to you and tell you to take a hike rather than keep lying to us. Jack, you've met your match. Stop fighting it. Go back over there and beg her forgiveness."

Jack shook his head. "Now's not the time. Her court case is Monday. She told me this has all been a distraction. Her clinic is her life's work and her shelter is her passion. I can't insert my needs before hers. I have to give her space, even if that's the last thing I want to do."

"Proving he loves her," Joyce said. "Saints be praised. Finally." She fanned herself, looked upward, and whispered a thank-you to God. "We can fix this."

Jack admitted the fact that scared him the most. For the first time in his life, he didn't have an answer. "I don't know how or even where to begin."

His mother covered his hand and squeezed tight, like she'd do whenever the tornado sirens went off when he was little. "Oh darling, don't worry. That's what we're here for."

Chapter Eleven

It snowed the day of Kat's court date. Not enough to make everything a brilliant shade of wintery bliss, but instead just enough to torment those who wanted a white Christmas. The snow's flurrying flakes turned everything gray, sloshy and slushy instead of white and wonderful.

Kat parked in a nearby garage, sidestepped the puddles on the stairwell, and managed to make it through security and into the courthouse with two minutes to spare. Amy Aiken, Kat's lawyer, stood there checking her phone, fingers flying. As she finished her text, she gave Kat an acknowledging nod. "There you are. Judge Harper is running right on time. We're up in fifteen minutes. Let's talk over here."

Amy led Kat to a wooden bench, and Kat sat. She had worn her best suit, a conservative blue number with a skirt that fell to her knees. Despite the coolness of the vast space, under her jacket Kat began to sweat. She twisted the ends of her silk scarf.

"Let me review how this is going to go," Amy began as she outlined the procedure and offered tips on what Kat should and shouldn't say. Then Amy checked her watch, announced it was time to go, and ushered Kat into the back of the courtroom where they watched the last few minutes of a personal injury settlement. During the brief moment between cases, people moved around. Some exited, others entered. The judge never left the bench.

Kat followed Amy to the defendant's table and sat nervously. She spread her hands out, memorizing the texture of the dark brown stained wood. *This was it.* She swallowed nerves, put her hands in her lap, and squeezed tight.

Suddenly a flurry of movement appeared to her front. "I need you to sign this," said a familiar voice. Jack's brother stood there in a custom suit, a document extended. He slid it across the table.

"What are you doing here?" The words came from Kat's lawyer, as Kat was speechless.

"Hi Amy," Matt said in reply. "I'm joining you."

Then he turned to Kat. "I'm entering on your behalf as co-counsel. Trust me. You need to sign this hiring me."

"Amy?" Kat asked. When Amy shrugged, Kat signed where indicated, uncertain as to what was going on.

"Perfect. Let me give this to the judge." He set his briefcase flat on the table and asked for permission to approach the bench. Judge Harper motioned him forward.

Matt returned. "Fill me in quickly," he said to Amy. "We have a few minutes."

As Amy and Matt began to confer, Kat turned around and surveyed the people in the courtroom. She craned her neck to scan the crowd, then turned back around and sat back with a thump.

None of this made any sense. Why was Matt here? Why was he helping her after she'd called things off with Jack and broken their deal? And where was Jack?

Judge Harper banged his gavel, and Kat jumped in her seat. She touched her throat, tried to calm down. The case had started.

Real courtrooms don't mimic TV dramas, and Fred Fennewald's lawyer went first, presenting all of the neighborhood association's grievances. As Fred took the stand and said his piece, Kat tried to tune everything out. His words were hateful and personal as he spoke out against her. Then Matt rose to his feet for the cross-examination.

"I wish you would have told me about this," Amy whispered. "If you wanted to replace me, you just had to speak up."

"I didn't," Kat insisted. "This is all Matt's idea. I had no idea he'd do this."

Amy appeared mollified. "Well, he's one of the best there is. I hate going up against him. Be glad he's on our side. He's a shark."

They watched as Matt decimated Fred, the judge overruling many of his lawyer's objections. Even though this wasn't a criminal trial, Matt still went about discrediting Fred, who appeared red and flustered by the time Matt said, "No more questions."

"You're up next," Amy told Kat, who wiped nervous hands on her skirt.

Matt returned to the defense table, poker-faced, and took a sip of water. "Defense calls Detective Jack Donovan."

"Didn't see *that* coming," Amy said. Kat agreed. Her heart soared, and then there he was, wearing his dress uniform, striding up the aisle and onto the witness stand.

She willed him to look at her, but he did no such thing. It didn't escape her that he'd come through, kept his end of their deal. *He'd done this for her.* He'd promised he'd help, and he had. He'd called in the ace—stepbrother Matt. She knew how much that must have cost him.

Kat's heart flatlined. She didn't deserve Jack. She'd treated him like dirt. She'd tossed him aside. *Oh God. What had she done? How could she ever make it up to him?*

Jack spoke clearly and confidently about Kat's shelter. He went on the record with all that he'd seen. He spoke about the pet adoption event and how to this date all the animals Kat had placed had found forever homes. Then he left the stand, giving Kat one professional glance as he strode by her. She twisted her neck for one last glimpse before he went out the big double doors.

"Am I up there next?" she asked, but Matt was in motion.

"Judge Harper, may I approach the bench? I'd like to present a letter from the mayor, a letter he wrote in support of Ms. Saunders's shelter."

Judge Harper waved Matt forward, took the letter, and read it aloud. Kat couldn't believe the contents. The letter reminded the court that the city did not fund its own shelters, and with the abundance of homeless animals, any regulation no-kill shelter of the quality of the Chippewa Animal Clinic should be welcome in the city, not closed. He also praised Kat's work with Jingle. When Judge Harper finished, he set the letter down and removed his reading glasses. Rubbed the bridge of his nose.

Then the judge gestured. "This is ridiculous. You heard the mayor's wishes, Mr. Banner. I would suggest you and Ms. Saunders reach a compromise designed to keep the character of the neighborhood all while happily coexisting with an animal shelter and clinic. Because I see no reason to continue this. I'm going to rule that the city grant the shelter permit effective immediately. However, I will give you ten days to mediate and find a harmonious relationship. In the spirit of the holidays and all."

Kevin Banner leaned over to confer with his Fred. "We'd be happy to find a solution," he said a moment later.

Amy stood. "My client would be happy to work with the neighborhood association as well."

Judge Harper banged his gavel. "Then schedule a date and time to make the peace before you leave. This case is dismissed. The city will issue a permit."

Kat felt giddy. She'd won.

"Thanks Matt," Amy said, shaking his hand. "I have it from here." She moved toward Kevin and Fred.

"I don't know how to thank you . . ." Kat began, rising

to her feet. "What do I owe you?"

"Nothing. I've got a busy day. I have to run. See you at Christmas." Matt grabbed his briefcase and left before she could stop him.

"What was that about Christmas?" Amy asked, returning. "You're going to his house for Christmas?"

"No. I'm as confused as you are."

She gave Kat a long look of disbelief. "Our mediation meeting is the first week of January. I'll send you an e-mail. Have a great holiday. You've earned it."

Kat thanked her lawyer, who headed for the exit, and stood there a moment before the next defendants approached the table. She grabbed her coat and exited, looking around the hallway as if Jack would suddenly appear.

But he didn't, and Kat drove back to her clinic. Even so he'd given her the best gift of all, her dream.

She was a fixer. She had to fix things between them.

***

Two days later, Christmas Eve, found Kat extremely frustrated. Jack hadn't answered her voice mails. He'd answered only one of her text messages: "No need to thank me. Busy. Promise we'll talk later."

And that had been that. He'd proved he kept his promises, but as minutes turned into hours and hours into days, Kat wondered when he'd call. She'd replayed every moment of their relationship in her head. She couldn't pinpoint the exact moment she'd fallen in love with him.

Had it been the night they'd saved Jingle? Or gone to the hockey game? Or when they stayed in and ended up in bed? Since the breakup, she'd watched every Hallmark movie on her DVR, crying at the end as she always did because she was happy, but now also for what she herself had lost. So she'd thrown herself into work.

"There you go." Kat lifted Jinx, now named Mr. Hugh, and returned him into Lizzy's outstretched arms. "He's all better, but we can't let him chew on any more plastic bags, either. Okay?"

"Thank you," Mrs. Schneider said. "I was worried."

"Well, you did the right thing bringing him in for a checkup," Kat said.

"He's such a great cat," Mrs. Schneider gushed as a vet tech helped Lizzy put a reluctant Mr. Hugh back in his cat carrier. "He sleeps with Lizzy every night. He's been a godsend."

"You have a great Christmas," Kat said. She watched them exit the exam room and walked back through to her office. It was Christmas Eve, and she was booked solid until noon, when the clinic hosted its annual party. Santa would arrive and pass out presents to neighborhood children and pets.

Kat had five minutes between patients and went back to check on Jingle. Almost a month had gone by, and he was progressing well. Not needing as many intensive painkillers, he was able to lift his head when she came to his side. "Hey Jingle," she said, and he licked her hand. "Aren't you a good boy?"

"The Kindreds are here." Louise approached. "The tech's in doing vitals now."

"Thank you." Kat gave Jingle one more pat.

"How are you doing?" Louise asked.

Kat gave the same answer she'd given since Monday. "Fine. We have our shelter."

"I meant with Jack."

"Oh," Kat said. He was constantly in her mind, but nothing she wanted to talk about.

"This is your favorite time of the year and you're miserable. We all hate it. We want you happy."

Kat adjusted her ponytail. An a cappella version of "O Christmas Tree" piped through the speakers, and Jingle seemed to sigh. She ran her hand along his head one last time before she met her next patient. "He likes Christmas music," Kat noted, shoving her right hand in her lab coat pocket, "and the Kindreds are waiting."

"Not an answer," Louise called.

Kat's spirits lifted as the clock inched toward noon. Like the pet adoption, this gala worked open-house style, with Santa arriving at twelve ten to distribute the presents. Many guests brought dogs sporting canine fashions from Santa hats and elf ears to sweaters embroidered with Christmas trees. "Looks like a great crowd," her partner, Dr. Marshall, said.

Kat agreed," letting the Christmas spirit invade. She loved this holiday and especially this party. Nothing would spoil it. So she made the rounds, passing out cookies and punch, petting dogs, and speaking with clients, until she realized Santa was running late. Angela had been in charge of the scheduling, as she'd done every December. Kat gave a quizzical glance, and Angela mouthed, "Don't worry."

Kat rolled her shoulders back and relaxed. Angela wouldn't fail to have secured a Santa, the event's very important guest. In fact, she now heard a jingling noise, a tinkling of bells, coming from the hallway.

"Ho ho ho!" a deep voice boomed as a white-bearded, jolly man in a red fat suit entered. He heaved a big red bag from his shoulder onto the floor in front of the Christmas tree. Children ran over, excitedly calling "Santa!" "Santa!"

Parents eased closer as Kat stood back, watching the mayhem. Louise, in an elf outfit, stood by Santa to help distribute presents. With the people in the way, she couldn't see or hear Santa's conversations, but clearly the kids liked whatever he said for she heard them squeal and laugh.

"Seems like we got a good Santa," Kat told Angela.

She nodded. "Oh yes, this one's special. Came highly recommended."

"We'll have to get him again next year."

"Play your cards right and that won't be a problem," Angela said. She turned to a young mother and child who wanted to purchase a dog collar. "Here, let me help you with that."

Kat leaned back against the counter, her white lab coat draping about her tan chinos. She lifted a cup of hot cocoa to her lips and wiped the whipped cream off her lip with a napkin. Strains of "Santa Claus Is Coming to Town" mixed with laughter, barking, and conversation. *Another successful event. And thanks to Jack, they'd keep coming.*

She pushed away the returning melancholy. The crowd thinned as people left, and she set her empty cup down. She walked toward the tree and stopped short. *She knew that voice.*

"Jack?"

"Nope," he chortled. He had a five-year-old on his lap. "She thinks I'm Jack Frost," he told the young girl, who giggled. "Do I look like Jack Frost?"

"No," the girl shrieked with glee. "You're Santa!"

"Of course, he is," Kat recovered, giving the little girl a wide, reassuring smile. Behind round wire spectacles, Jack's blue eyes twinkled. "Santa always makes a stop here before he starts his sleigh rides," Kat said.

"He likes to see the doggies," the little girl said with an all-knowing nod.

"Yes, I do," Jack said in his deep Santa voice. He tickled the girl's arm and she giggled. Then he set her on the floor and she raced back to her parents, who'd finished taking pictures on their smart phones. She held up her candy cane and her present—a doll Kat had purchased at Five Below. These weren't huge presents, but the kids didn't care about the value, they cared about the experience.

"Thank you for doing this," the mother told Kat before they left, their well-behaved Doberman at their heels. "We just moved into the neighborhood and I'm so glad to find you. We'll bring Brutus in for his yearly checkup next week."

"I'm glad to meet you," Kat replied

She faced Jack, who'd welcomed another child onto Santa's lap, keeping them from speaking. She watched him for the briefest moment, before being called away by one of her clients who wanted to say good-bye. What was he doing here? And in a Santa suit, no less?

"How did you do it?" she asked Angela at five minutes to one. The event would clearly run over.

"You mean get Santa?" Angela smirked.

"No, Jack. He hates Christmas."

"You'll have to ask him. It was all his idea."

Kat frowned. "That makes no sense."

"Call it a Christmas mystery . . . or miracle," Angela said, but before Kat could press her further, a customer who'd decided to buy a Thunder Shirt for her dog captured Angela's attention.

Kat waited by the counter for when she could talk to Jack. At last the clinic cleared, and Angela locked the front door. The lobby quieted, except for staff conversations and the music piping through the speakers.

Santa was on his feet, and Kat headed over. "Jack. Wait."

"Ho ho ho. Santa's late." He reached into his sack and withdrew a red envelope. "However, Santa would love for you to read this."

"Jack."

But instead he left, leaving her standing there holding the envelope. She turned it over in her hands, feeling the smooth texture and noting the round gold seal where the back flap reached a point. She slipped the greeting card into her coat pocket as Dr. Marshall came back so they could give their staff their holiday bonuses. As Christmas was on a Thursday, the clinic would be closed until the day after, excepting emergencies, of course.

"Aren't you going to open it?" Angela asked later, after the staff party. Around Kat, the staff bustled about, cleaning up.

"I will." Kat grabbed a garbage bag and began clearing away residual trash. While the card had been burning a hole in her pocket, she hadn't wanted to read it until she had time to be alone. The right time came thirty minutes later, when she finally sat down at her desk around three o'clock.

She slid her finger under the heavy paper, the ensuing tear creating a jagged edge at the top. She pulled out a glossy white card, which read simply Merry Christmas in red embossed lettering above a green fir tree with red ball ornaments. *It looked like her tree.*

She slid her finger under the edge, opening the card sideways to her left. A piece of cardstock fluttered out, and Kat made a grab for it, noted it was a ticket to the Mayor's Black & White Ball, and set it aside. The inside of the card was also white, and the red printing read "Wishing You a Wonderful Holiday and Happy New Year."

But it was what was underneath, in Jack's black-ink scrawl, that captured her attention. "Let's start this over," he'd written. "Are you willing to attend one more event? I'd love it if you say yes. J."

She looked at the ticket to the Black & White Ball, one of the most exclusive New Year's Eve invitations in the city. The dress code was formal—black or white tuxedos and women in black or white dresses, or a combination of the two. She'd heard the event was like something out of Hollywood. If she went, she'd need to buy a dress, and the part of her that loved retail therapy thrilled at the idea.

Plus it meant spending New Year's Eve with Jack, instead of drinking a glass of sparkling wine with her cats and watching the ball drop in New York City on TV.

She turned the ticket over between her fingers. He'd sent one. Did that mean she meet him there?

She hated mysteries about as much as she hated games, although she was certain this was the former, not the latter.

Her stomach grumbled as Kat rose. She'd figure out what to do at home. She planned on attending nine o'clock Christmas morning mass, which meant she needed to be up early to could check on Jingle and the other animals first. Since it was Christmas, Kat, not one of her employees would go in.

She did the final check of the clinic and left around four o'clock, darkness beginning to blanket the city. A storm front had rolled in, and the weathermen were predicting two inches of powdery snow to fall tonight, enough to make everything magical without coating streets and paralyzing traffic. The moist, blustery air certainly felt like snow, she thought as she climbed into her car. She picked up some Chinese food and carried that and the bag of presents her employees had given her up the stairs. Her tenants had gone to Kansas City for the holiday, so she'd house sit their two cats, feeding them first thing tomorrow.

She flipped the lights on, and was enthusiastically greeted by Pippa and Ty, who rubbed in between her legs in the hopes of securing some of the meat from her beef and broccoli order. She sidestepped them, set the bags on the counter, and brought her dinner out into the living room, where she first watched *Jeopardy*, the local news, and then *NBC Nightly News with Brian Williams*.

As the next local news broadcast began, Kat sighed and checked out the offerings on Netflix. Tonight she'd normally be with her parents or some of her friends, but everyone was out of town, and with being so busy at work, she hadn't made any arrangements to do something productive, like volunteer to serve dinner at the one of the homeless shelters.

There were worse things than being alone, but being alone on Christmas sucked.

Her front doorbell buzzed, and Kat set her plate of half-eaten dinner down on the coffee table, to the delight of the hovering cats with the twitchy noses.

A group of shadows stood outside her door, and as she got closer she heard a chorus of voices. Christmas carolers. She turned on the front porch light.

As she opened the heavy wooden door, the chorus grew louder as the group of men and women and children began "God rest ye merry gentlemen, let nothing you dismay, remember Christ our savior was born on

Christmas Day . . ."

Wind swirled in around her slipper-covered feet, but Kat didn't feel cold. They sang the complete song, then began "Silent Night."

As the song came to an end, Kat realized she didn't have any money. "Let me run upstairs and . . ."

A round, pink-cheeked woman put out her gloved hand. In it was a green envelope. "Oh no, ma'am. No money. We're the City Players and we carol for charity. We received a donation to come by your house. We're to give you this."

Kat took the offered envelope. "Thank you." She stood there awkwardly. "Are you sure I can't get you anything? Hot cocoa? Replenish your coffee?"

The woman shook her head. "Thank you but we must be off to our next stop if we're to keep our schedule. You have a blessed Christmas."

"And a Happy New Year," someone else called, which was echoed by the others, and with that the group shuffled down the sidewalk to enter two huge passenger vans.

Kat closed her front door and shuffled back upstairs. She flopped on the couch, movie choices frozen and waiting on the TV screen. She tore into the envelope. This card was white like the other, but the outside had a gold embossed trumpet, complete with decorative holly, that almost completely filled the five-by-seven horizontal space. She lifted the flap, and the inside read "May Your Christmas Be Filled with Joyful Noise."

There was just a J for a signature.

And with that, Kat burst into tears.

Chapter Twelve

Sitting across the street and parked slightly down from Kat's, Jack watched the carolers leave. Had she liked them? Was his plan even working?

He'd never done anything so crazy, but his mother the expert matchmaker insisted he follow her instructions to the letter. Still, he'd itched to answer Kat's texts and voice mails. But Mike, now his full-time partner and the second member of the task force, stood as a testament to Joyce's abilities. Jack had to trust his mom knew best. So he sat in a darkened car with his sister Brenna, who looked over at him.

"Okay, it's time. Get out and go."

"You're sure about this?"

She shrugged and started the car. "I'm nineteen. I have no idea. But Mom is legendary, and you agreed to play along. So out."

Jack reached for the door handle of Brenna's compact. He'd folded himself inside, and getting out seemed even more painful. He'd left his SUV in his parents' driveway. Normally he'd be in the old neighborhood tonight, for his mother and Nelson always hosted a Christmas Eve open house that lasted until everyone went to midnight mass.

"So, she's the one, huh?"

Jack pulled his down parka tighter. A few snow flurries had started to fall, and being without a car was a calculated risk, one his mother had insisted upon. "We'll come get you if it fails," she'd announced. "But it won't."

He clutched the gold envelope in his left hand and pulled the door handle with his right. *Now or never. Stand or fall.*

Boot hit curb, and as soon as he'd closed the passenger door, Brenna was off like a bullet. Jack inhaled a deep breath, his exhale creating a misty white cloud. He crossed the street and went up to the house covered in Christmas lights and holiday inflatables. Frosty the Snowman gave Jack a friendly wave, which Jack hoped was a good omen. He'd live with this memory the rest of his life.

He prayed it'd be a good one.

***

Kat sniffled and wiped her eyes on her sleeve. Was that the doorbell again? She grabbed a napkin from the takeout order and blew her nose. The cats had eaten some of the beef and licked the sauce clean, avoiding the broccoli like children do. Unlike the cats at the clinic, Kat's home cats weren't as well trained. She knew she shouldn't have let them eaten people food, but this one time would be okay. She didn't have time to check her face, and as she went downstairs, she hoped her eyes weren't too red and puffy. She'd left the porch light on, and she could see one silhouette through the stained glass insert. She unlocked the door and drank in the man she loved, then had lost because of her own stupidity and fear. "Jack."

"Hey, I wanted to give you this—" his words stopped cold as he took in her appearance. He shoved something in his coat pocket. "You've been crying."

"I'm fine," Kat lied. *Wallowing in self-pity, yes. Fine, no.*

He used his left forefinger to wipe away a stray tear, the tip turning black. Kat saw it. "Oh no! I must look like a raccoon!" She turned and fled back up the stairs, leaving Jack to close and lock the door. He turned off the porch light. Well, she hadn't kicked him out on sight. That was a good sign, right?

He unzipped his coat as he climbed the stairs. She wasn't in the living room, and he noted the suspiciously clean, abandoned plate, the scrunched napkin, and the oyster pail still half full of white sticky rice. She'd poured a glass of water, and the ice was partially melted. She'd been perusing romantic Christmas movies, he noted, although in the recently viewed column he saw the poster for the first *Die Hard*. He smiled at that. Yes, she was the woman of his heart. He shoved his gloves into his coat and draped that over the back of a chair. Pippa instantly claimed the garment by positioning herself dead center, curling up for a nap.

Michele Dunaway

Kat returned, sans the fuzzy pink slippers she'd been wearing. And she'd wiped down her face. "Jack. What are you doing here?"

He heard the slight tremble in her voice, imperceptible to anyone but him, for he knew her, and wanted to know her forever.

"I wanted to deliver this one personally," he said.

Kat took the gold envelope from his outstretched hand. "Thank you."

She stood there awkwardly.

"Why were you crying?" He asked. "Did I make you cry?"

"No. The carolers—"

"Were my idea."

"They were lovely. I'm just melancholy this holiday. Normally I have this huge routine and—"

"Open the card."

"You're keeping Hallmark in business," Kat quipped, trying for a bravado she didn't feel. He was larger than life, standing there in fitted Levi's and a deep burgundy, chamois flannel long-sleeved shirt. "Why are you doing this?"

"What?" he asked.

"Being so nice to me. I was a jerk. I called off our deal. Yet you kept up your end. I'm a heel." Tears threatened.

"Open the card," Jack urged.

So Kat stuck her finger under the flap and gave a little cry as the paper sliced across the pad, giving her a paper cut. "Oh! Ow." She pulled back her finger and stuck it in her mouth.

"Let me see." Jack gently took her hand and tenderly examined her finger. "Let's put a bandage on it. Do you have any?"

"Bathroom."

He led her into the small space, where he washed her hand in the sink, dried it, and then expertly applied a small adhesive bandage, which wrapped all around her finger. Her body quivered from the intimacy of his actions. She'd missed his touch. *Missed him.*

He guided her back into the living room, sat her on the couch. "Love *Die Hard*. We should watch it sometime," he told her, retrieving the envelope that had cut her. He removed the card and handed it over. "Here. "

This card was vertical like the first one, and like the other two, it was also white. A beautiful embossed angel decorated the front, complete with golden wings and a silvery halo. Kat opened the card, and as she did, a green bone-shaped dog tag fell into her lap. "Leave it," Jack said, so she did, and instead read the words on the card: "Joy. Joy. Joy. Wishing You Endless Joy."

He hadn't signed this one, but simply written "I'm sorry."

She glanced up to find him staring at her intently. "Me too."

He drew her into his arms. "I botched things."

"No, I did."

"You are perfect."

"Hardly. I left you high and dry."

"It was the jolt I needed."

"Then why didn't you answer my messages?"

"I wanted to give us time to think. To have a break. To be able to make a fresh start. One not based in lies."

"Jack."

"Shh," he told her, placing a finger on her lips. She loved his touch. "New year. New start. Until then, it's Christmas. So ask me what we're going to do."

Her heart soared. "Okay, I'll bite. What are we doing?"

"Attending my mom's Christmas Eve open house."

Part of her deflated. "I'm not up for company and you no longer need a fake date."

"No, I don't. I confessed everything to my family. The only thing I need is you. Just you."

She reached into her lap, pulled out the dog tag. It read simply "Jingle." Even though Jingle wouldn't wear a collar for a long time, the small gesture touched her. "Why me?"

"Because I love you."

His words brought tears to her eyes, and she turned the dog tag over, memorizing the etching as a way to keep her composure. Part of her so wanted to believe him! But the practical part couldn't let go yet. Couldn't risk. "This is sweet. I'll hang it on his cage. Thank you. Thanks for all of this."

"Oh Kat, you're welcome. I wanted your holiday to be special. I promised you that, and I want to make your dreams come true. Please give us another chance."

"Jack . . ." Her heart overflowed as did her tears. He hugged her closer.

"Shh. No more tears. From here on out, it's going to be fine. So come with me tonight. It's a huge party that ends when everyone leaves for midnight mass, and I want you there not because it's a deal, but because I can't imagine being there without you. I want you in my life."

She leaned into him, needing the physical connection they'd always shared. "We can't skip it?"

He moved back. "I'm not allowed to take you to bed."

"What?"

"Mom's rules. She says I'm to woo you since I've failed to do that. I want to do things right, Kat. I want to fix my terrible track record."

Wooing sounded wonderful. Sincerity and love—she could read both on Jack's face. She fingered her clothes. It would take her only five minutes to change. He played his ace. "Besides, my sister dropped me off. My car was boxed in. I need a ride back."

"Oh Jack." She sighed, realizing his mother was one smart customer. "Really?"

He grinned, spread his hands out on his legs. "Mom's idea. I'm new at this wooing. So please? If you're really opposed, you can just throw me out the car door. But it's Christmas Eve and Bruce Willis can wait."

True. However . . . "I always watch for Alan Rickman."

Jack smiled, and it tugged her heartstrings. "He does make a good villain."

"Snape, Sheriff of Nottingham. Yep. But I like him as Colonel Brandon too."

He tilted his head, exposing a line of five-o'clock shadow. "I don't know who that is."

She laughed. "You mean your sister didn't make you watch *Pride and Prejudice?*"

He shuddered. "No. My man card didn't punch that one."

"Promise to watch it with me."

"If I do, will you come? You'll have your car. You can leave any time."

She considered her options. Pippa was curled up on Jack's coat, napping away. Ty lay on the floor near the heat register, belly stretched toward the sky. Jack had gone through all this trouble. And she loved Christmas. Being alone was not appealing. "If it gets your mom off your back, I can go for a little while," she capitulated. "Let me go get ready."

"Great." Jack waited until Kat had disappeared into her bedroom to send a group message: "Ten minutes."

Then he relocated Pippa and put on his coat, and soon he and Kat were on their way. He had more wooing to do.

***

"Kat!" Joyce greeted as soon as she and Jack stepped into the crowded house. "I'm so glad you came."

"Thank you for inviting me."

"Of course. Now Jack, put her coat on the bed and get

her something to drink."

"Yes ma'am," Jack replied.

Kat had to admit she enjoyed the party. No one mentioned her and Jack's troubles, as if there was a prearranged force field around the topic. Instead, people asked about her shelter, inquired after Jingle, and discussed how Kat liked being a vet. She met Mike, Jack's partner, and his wife Suze and she liked them both.

Hours passed quickly, and suddenly it was eleven thirty and people were leaving, heading to mass at Our Lady of Sorrows. "Let's skip mass," she told Jack. "My plan was to go in the morning."

"How about I follow you home?" Jack wrapped her coat around her as she slid her arms inside. They stepped out into a world of softly falling flakes. It would be a white Christmas after all.

She drove the ten minutes journey slowly; the roads passable if traveled carefully. Jack parked in her driveway and waited as she closed the garage door.

Then as they walked through the back gate, she stopped short. She'd installed a lot of Christmas lights, but now there were more. Thousands more. Spiral Christmas trees lined her sidewalk with waves of small twinkling lights draped between. The effect was a magical fairy walk. "Did you do this?"

"How could I? I was with you."

"Jack. This must have cost a fortune."

"I want you happy, Kat. I want this to be your best Christmas ever."

"You keep making me cry. This is why you had to get me out of the house."

"Partially," Jack replied. "There's more though." He handed her another card.

"Jack."

"Doesn't a greeting card say it best?"

As they stood in her well-lit, magical backyard, Kat slid her non-injured finger underneath. This card was white like the rest but with a green embossed wreath. The green words inside read "A wish for peace and happiness at Christmas and throughout the New Year."

Underneath Jack had written, "and all the years after that. For I love you Kat, and we're going to make this work."

The last term of endearment hit her hard. A warm, fuzzy feeling blossomed and she didn't even feel the gentle snowfall. Hope bloomed. Jack had given her Christmas magic. Mister-I'm-Not-a-Fan-of-Christmas had sent her a magical ticket, given a gift to the dog she'd saved, serenaded her with carolers, and made sure she hadn't been alone when she'd been feeling down. He'd restored her faith, revived her spirit.

"Let me tell you how this is going to go," he said. "I love you. I've only known you a short time, but my mother says you know your soul mate. Cecily insists that you simply know, and for the first time, I can say with absolute certainty that I do.

"I've waited my whole life to find you, and I'm not going to let you go. Not again. I made a mistake not telling you how my feelings had changed. Now I stand here and hope you somehow, someday will love me back."

If hearts could overflow, hers was. "Oh Jack." She reached for him. "I already do."

"Then I'm the luckiest guy in the world."

He brought his lips down to hers, kissing her under the softly falling Christmas snow for what seemed like sweet eternity. Down the road church chimes counted off midnight. His lips left hers. "Merry Christmas, Kat."

"Merry Christmas, Jack." She leaned back, secure in his arms, and put her hand out to catch the falling snow. "I love white Christmases."

"And I love you. I promise you will always know how much."

"That'll be the best present of all."

"Better than this?" He pulled a small red box out from his pocket, flipped it open. Inside nestled a beautiful Christmas-themed ring with red, green, and white stones. "When I saw this, I thought of you."

"It's a beautiful." Her exhale vaporized in the cold.

"It's a promise ring. I promise you I'm serious about us. Serious about our future. I love you, Kat."

"I love you too. I'm so happy. Does it get better than this?"

"I promise it will."

"Then let's go inside." She held out her hand. Waited.

"My mom said—"

Kat laughed, grabbed his hand, and tugged him to her. She kissed him hard, until she'd stolen his breath away.

"On this I'm overruling your mother. After all, you're mine now."

"I like the sound of that."

"Me too."

So Jack let her pull him along, under the canopy of twinkling lights, to their first of many Christmases.

Epilogue

One year later

The Missouri Botanical Garden was a plethora of lights, its annual holiday garden glow in full swing. Thousands of lights adorned some of the garden's most famous exhibits, like the Climatron, the Kaeser Memorial Maze, and the Tower Grove House.

Monsanto Hall had been set aglow as well, venue for the annual Pet Rescue gala.

". . . so ladies and gentlemen, Detective Jack Donovan," Jeff Ellis introduced.

"You'll be fine," Kat whispered, giving him a kiss on the cheek.

Jack stood up and walked to the podium. At his heels trotted the real guest of honor, Jingle. The dog had made great strides. Since February, Jack and Kat had been teaching him simple commands. In mid-March, they'd become Jingle's foster parents. They'd officially adopted him the day after Thanksgiving, one year to the day he'd been found.

Jack leaned down and patted Jingle on the head. He adjusted the bow around the dog's neck. Jingle sat quietly next to the podium, the camera projecting his image on the big screen.

Jack began his speech, outlining Jingle's care. The screen displayed a slideshow of pictures, from the horrific beginning through the laser treatments to a shot of Jingle curled up with Pippa. As the show ended, the screen shot again went live.

"Because of the task force, Jingle has his forever home. But it took the work of people like you, donors and Animal Cruelty Task Force partners. It also involved one special person." Jack looked at the table where his parents, Kat's parents, Matt and Sharon, Brian and Cecily sat with Kat.

The slide behind him changed, and he saw Kat frown as she read the words that said "Kat, say this." But she trusted Jack and followed the directions, calling her pet. "Jingle. Come."

Unleashed when Jack had adjusted his collar, Jingle gave one bark and trotted over to his beloved mistress. As he sat before her, Kat noticed the little something shiny Jack had attached to the red and green tartan Christmas bow tied to his collar, a bow that hid some of the scars he'd always have.

The screen read "Kat, will you marry me?" but the podium was empty as Jack had moved to kneel at Kat's side. Trembling fingers undid the ring. "Kat, I love you.

Will you marry me?" he asked.

"Yes. Oh yes."

Stronger fingers slid the solitaire on her finger. The camera zoomed in, and Jack and Kat were broadcast to everyone in the hall. Jingle barked again.

"Saints be praised," Jack's mother Joyce said as everyone in the hall clapped.

"I love you Kat," Jack whispered as they stood and Jack held up her hand for all to see.

"And I love you."

The band began to play, and people moved around them, toward the dance floor. Jingle barked. "Shall we get him out of here?" Jack asked.

"Absolutely," Kat answered, as Jingle, sensing his advantage, wrapped the leash around her ankles, pressing Kat into the man she loved. She laughed and gave Jack a kiss filled with the promise of all the nights to come. "I want you alone anyway."

Sneak Peak of
Mr. July

Prologue

The sun wasn't supposed to be shining on days like this. Rain would have been better—big, dark and stormy rain clouds would at least have matched Brad's anger and ire. Hard-slapping raindrops would also hide any slip of emotion, although men stoic in their Navy dress blues didn't shed tears. Yet the fight to hold them back was one of the hardest-fought battles of his life. A seagull took flight, finding his friends so they could play on the warm ocean breeze that blew across Coronado and made its way gently across the bay to San Diego. The breeze made the mid-eighties day perfectly palatable. Already Todd's elderly parents had been waiting over forty minutes for the Navy chaplain to begin the service, but Father Joseph couldn't begin until the casket arrived.

That was still a hundred yards away, being slowly carried along the assigned route.

Brad stood at attention, sweating under the dark uniform that locked in the heat. He waited at the end of the line, the pallbearers made up of the current members of Todd's SEAL team, a role Brad had forfeited when he'd turned down the promotion. Brad had opted out of the transfer, and once his six-year enlistment ended, he'd head back to St. Louis. Todd had signed back up without any hesitation or backward glances. There'd been no talking him out of staying a SEAL. Less than a year later, his best friend was dead.

Brad could still remember the conversation when he'd told his friend—both he and Todd at a local dive, sharing a pitcher of beer over several games of pool. Todd was between overseas deployments, training for the mission ahead.

"You were finally going to be on my team. The guys and I were ready for it." Todd had taken a deep drink of the sudsy draft. Brad could still picture how he'd had to wipe his lip of the foam.

"Couldn't do it," Brad admitted. "I wish you'd followed me out."

"Thought about it. But I'm not cut out for civilian life. My country needs me."

"Scarlett needs you. She loves you."

"Yeah. But trust me, she understands." Todd drank more beer. Turned serious. "I need you to do me a solid. A favor. I'm shipping out in a few weeks."

On the same mission Brad would also have been on, had he chosen to say yes. "Anything, man. What are friends for?"

"Good. I know I can trust you. You've always had my back. Got a letter. For Scarlett. Should something happen. Gonna snail mail it to you. I hope you'll never need it, but if you do, give it to her when the time's right."

Scarlett. Todd's wife. Brad's secret high school crush. But once Todd had called dibs, that had been that. Brad had stood as best man at Todd and Scarlett's wedding. Tried to forget how he felt about her. Told himself that thinking he was in love with her was nothing but a stupid obsession. A weakness to overcome. Something that would change when he found "the one." Only the one had never shown up, and his feelings hadn't changed. No woman compared.

The breeze shifted and Brad ignored the discomfort of standing at attention this long. On missions, he'd sat quiet and still for hours, but this was different, and the pain was wearing him down. He'd received the package a few weeks after that night in the bar, and inside was a sealed envelope addressed to Scarlett, along with some handwritten, one-page notes addressed to Brad upon which Todd had scrawled his last wishes—detailed instructions that Brad would now follow with military precision. In a twist of irony, today would be his last day in uniform. Tomorrow he'd fly back to his base, pack his things, and move home.

The honor guard carrying the casket came into sight. Behind, Scarlett walked, her certain step and emotionless expression designed to hide her grief. Brad could hear the thumps now, the sound of metal hitting the top of the casket as each of Todd's naval brethren removed his trident and set the metal badge atop the casket. The rhythmic thumping got louder as the casket came closer. "There's Mommy," he heard Todd's two-year-old daughter say. She was too young to fully understand what was going on and too small to walk the distance. "Shh," Todd's mother soothed, holding Colleen tight.

Brad straightened further as the trident-covered casket came within his reach. The pallbearers slowed, and with a thump, Brad added his own trident. Then they went past and up onto the dais, where dignitaries waited to honor the life of a SEAL gone too soon, but one whose heroic actions had saved the lives in his unit. Like precision clockwork, everyone moved into place and the service started.

Brad had seen Scarlett briefly last night after he'd flown in. Todd's parents wanted him buried in St. Louis, but Scarlett had relayed those weren't his wishes. Instead, inside the rental casket was an urn containing his ashes. Brad's gaze caught hers, and he shot the full force of his sympathy toward her. She was a proud woman, Todd had warned in the missives he'd sent. She would resist all outside help. But Todd had given Brad a job. Thought his best friend could somehow succeed in helping when all others failed, as Todd clearly believed they would.

Brad stared at the casket, at Todd's weeping parents, and at the drained, sad face of Todd's wife. Scarlett. No amount of telling her he was sorry would help now. He might be leaving the Navy, but he had to complete this last mission as assigned.

He owed it to his friend.

He owed it to his friend's daughter.

And he especially owed it to Scarlett.

The fact they were here today was entirely his fault.

Acknowledgments

For my fans, who've stayed with me for 20 years, and for my own daughters, who mean the world. While places in the book are real, they've been fictionalized and are in no means representative of real people or circumstances.

About the Author

Describing herself as a woman who does way too much and never wants to stop, Michele Dunaway is a bestselling author and award-winning high school English teacher. Proud mother of two daughters, Michele is an avid pet lover who shares her home with far too many rescued cats, who of course completely rule the roost.